WAR AND PEACE

FIRST EPILOGUE : 1813 - 20

By Leo Tolstoy

Double 9
BOOKS

War and Peace
FIRST EPILOGUE : 1813 - 20
By Leo Tolstoy

ISBN: 978-93-94973-13-8

Published by

DOUBLE 9 BOOKS

2/13-B, Ansari Road
Daryaganj, New Delhi - 110002
info@double9books.com
www.double9books.com
Tel. 011-40042856

Printed in India.

About the Author

Leo Tolstoy was a Russian creator known for his books War and Peace which is viewed as the best book of pragmatist fiction. Tolstoy is additionally viewed as world's best author by quite a few people. Additionally an ethical scholar and a social reformer, Tolstoy had extreme moralistic points of view. In later life, he turned into an intense Christian rebel and anarcho-conservative.

Leo Tolstoy Born in Yasnaya Polyana on September 9, 1828, He had a place with a notable honorable Russian family. He was the fourth among five offspring of Count Nikolai Ilyich Tolstoy and Countess Mariya Tolstaya, both of whom kicked the bucket passing on their youngsters to be raised by family members.

In 1844, Tolstoy was acknowledged into Kazan University. Incapable to graduate past the subsequent year, Tolstoy got back to Yasnava Polyana and afterward invested energy going among Moscow and St. Petersburg. With some functioning information on a few dialects, he turned into a multilingual. Yet again the recently observed youth pulled in Tolstoy towards drinking, visiting massage parlors and most betting which left him in weighty obligation and anguish however Tolstoy before long acknowledged he was carrying on with a brutish life and endeavored college tests with the expectation that he would acquire a situation with the public authority, yet finished yet up in Caucuses serving in the military continuing in the strides of his senior sibling.

In Year 1862, Leo Tolstoy wedded Sophia Andreevna Behrs, generally called Sonya, who was 16 years more youthful than him. The couple had thirteen youngsters, of which, five passed on at an early age. Sonya went about as Tolstoy's secretary, editor and monetary chief while he made two out of his most prominent works. Their initial wedded life was loaded up with happiness. He started composing his show-stopper, War and Peace in 1862. The six volumes of the work were distributed somewhere in the range of 1863 and 1869. With 580 characters got from history and others made by Tolstoy, this extraordinary novel takes on investigating the hypothesis of history and the irrelevance of noted figures like Alexander and Napoleon. Anna Karenina, Tolstoy's next epic was begun in 1873 and distributed totally in 1878.

Contents

FIRST EPILOGUE : 1813 - 20

CHAPTER I

S even years had passed. The storm-tossed sea of European history had subsided within its shores and seemed to have become calm. But the mysterious forces that move humanity (mysterious because the laws of their motion are unknown to us) continued to operate. Though the surface of the sea of history seemed motionless, the movement of humanity went on as unceasingly as the flow of time. Various groups of people formed and dissolved, the coming formation and dissolution of kingdoms and displacement of peoples was in course of preparation.

The sea of history was not driven spasmodically from shore to shore as previously. It was seething in its depths. Historic figures were not borne by the waves from one shore to another as before. They now seemed to rotate on one spot. The historical figures at the head of armies, who formerly reflected the movement of the masses by ordering wars, campaigns, and battles, now reflected the restless movement by political and diplomatic combinations, laws, and treaties.

The historians call this activity of the historical figures "the reaction."

In dealing with this period they sternly condemn the historical personages who, in their opinion, caused what they describe as *the reaction*. All the well-known people of that period, from Alexander and Napoleon to Madame de Staël, Photius, Schelling, Fichte, Chateaubriand, and the rest, pass before their stern judgment seat and are acquitted or condemned according to whether they conduced to *progress* or to *reaction*.

According to their accounts a reaction took place at that time in Russia also, and the chief culprit was Alexander I, the same man who according to them was the chief cause of the liberal movement at the commencement of his reign, being the savior of Russia.

There is no one in Russian literature now, from schoolboy essayist to learned historian, who does not throw his little stone at Alexander for things he did wrong at this period of his reign.

"He ought to have acted in this way and in that way. In this case he did well and in that case badly. He behaved admirably at the beginning of his reign and during 1812, but acted badly by giving a constitution to Poland, forming the Holy Alliance, entrusting power to Arakchéev, favoringGolítsyn and mysticism, and afterwards Shishkóv and Photius. He also acted badly by concerning himself with the active army and disbanding the Semënov regiment."

It would take a dozen pages to enumerate all the reproaches the historians address to him, based on their knowledge of what is good for humanity.

What do these reproaches mean?

Do not the very actions for which the historians praise Alexander I (the liberal attempts at the beginning of his reign, his struggle with Napoleon, the firmness he displayed in 1812 and the campaign of 1813) flow from the same sources—the circumstances of his birth, education, and life—that made his personality what it was and from which the actions for which they blame him (the Holy Alliance, the restoration of Poland, and the reaction of 1820 and later) also flowed?

In what does the substance of those reproaches lie?

It lies in the fact that an historic character like Alexander I, standing on the highest possible pinnacle of human power with the blinding light of history focused upon him; a character exposed to those strongest of all influences: the intrigues, flattery, and self-deception inseparable from power; a character who at every moment of his life felt a responsibility for all that was happening in Europe; and not a fictitious but a live character who like every man had his personal habits, passions, and impulses toward goodness, beauty, and truth—that this character—though not lacking in virtue (the historians do not accuse him of that)—had not the same conception of the welfare of humanity fifty years ago as a present-day professor who from his youth upwards has been occupied with learning: that is, with books and lectures and with taking notes from them.

But even if we assume that fifty years ago Alexander I was mistaken in his view of what was good for the people, we must inevitably assume that the historian who judges Alexander will also after the lapse of some time turn out to be mistaken in his view of what is good for humanity. This assumption is all the more natural and inevitable because, watching the movement of history, we see that every year and with each new writer, opinion as to what is good for mankind changes; so that what once seemed good, ten years later seems bad, and vice versa. And what is more, we find at one and the same time quite contradictory views as to what is bad and what is good in history: some people regard giving a constitution to Poland and forming the Holy Alliance as praiseworthy in Alexander, while others regard it as blameworthy.

The activity of Alexander or of Napoleon cannot be called useful or harmful, for it is impossible to say for what it was useful or harmful. If that activity displeases somebody, this is only because it does not agree with his limited understanding of what is good. Whether the preservation of my father's house in Moscow, or the glory of the Russian arms, or the prosperity of the Petersburg and other universities, or the freedom of Poland or the greatness of Russia, or the balance of power in Europe, or a certain kind of European culture called "progress" appear to me to be good or bad, I must admit that besides these things the action of every historic character has other more general purposes inaccessible to me.

But let us assume that what is called science can harmonize all contradictions and possesses an unchanging standard of good and bad by which to try historic characters and events; let us say that Alexander could have done everything differently; let us say that with guidance from those who blame him and who profess to know the ultimate aim of the movement of humanity, he might have arranged matters according to the program his present accusers would have given him—of nationality, freedom, equality, and progress (these, I think, cover the ground). Let us assume that this program was possible and had then been formulated, and that Alexander had acted on it. What would then have become of the activity of all those who opposed the tendency that then prevailed in the government—an activity that in the opinion of the historians was good and beneficent? Their activity would not have existed: there would have been no life, there would have been nothing.

If we admit that human life can be ruled by reason, the possibility of life is destroyed.

CHAPTER II

I f we assume as the historians do that great men lead humanity to the attainment of certain ends—the greatness of Russia or of France, the balance of power in Europe, the diffusion of the ideas of the Revolution, general progress, or anything else—then it is impossible to explain the facts of history without introducing the conceptions of *chance* and *genius*.

If the aim of the European wars at the beginning of the nineteenth century had been the aggrandizement of Russia, that aim might have been accomplished without all the preceding wars and without the invasion. If the aim was the aggrandizement of France, that might have been attained without the Revolution and without the Empire. If the aim was the dissemination of ideas, the printing press could have accomplished that much better than warfare. If the aim was the progress of civilization, it is easy to see that there are other ways of diffusing civilization more expedient than by the destruction of wealth and of human lives.

Why did it happen in this and not in some other way?

Because it happened so! "*Chance* created the situation; *genius* utilized it," says history.

But what is *chance?* What is *genius?*

The words *chance* and *genius* do not denote any really existing thing and therefore cannot be defined. Those words only denote a certain stage of understanding of phenomena. I do not know why a certain event occurs; I think that I cannot know it; so I do not try to know it and I talk about *chance.* I see a force producing effects beyond the scope of ordinary human agencies; I do not understand why this occurs and I talk of *genius*.

To a herd of rams, the ram the herdsman drives each evening into a special enclosure to feed and that becomes twice as fat as the others must seem to be a genius. And it must appear an astonishing conjunction of genius with a whole series of extraordinary chances that this ram, who instead of getting into the general fold every evening goes into a special enclosure where there are oats—that this very ram, swelling with fat, is killed for meat.

But the rams need only cease to suppose that all that happens to them happens solely for the attainment of their sheepish aims; they need only admit that what happens to them may also have purposes beyond their ken, and they will at once perceive a unity and coherence in what happened to the ram that was fattened. Even if they do not know for what purpose they are fattened, they will at least know that all that happened to the ram did not happen accidentally, and will no longer need the conceptions of *chance* or *genius*.

Only by renouncing our claim to discern a purpose immediately intelligible to us, and admitting the ultimate purpose to be beyond our ken, may we discern the sequence of experiences in the lives of historic characters and perceive the cause of the effect they produce (incommensurable with ordinary human capabilities), and then the words *chance* and *genius* become superfluous.

We need only confess that we do not know the purpose of the European convulsions and that we know only the facts—that is, the murders, first in France, then in Italy, in Africa, in Prussia, in Austria, in Spain, and in Russia—and that the movements from the west to the east and from the east to the west form the essence and purpose of these events, and not only shall we have no need to see exceptional ability and genius in Napoleon and Alexander, but we shall be unable to consider them to be anything but like other men, and we shall not be obliged to have recourse to *chance* for an explanation of those small events which made these people what they were, but it will be clear that all those small events were inevitable.

By discarding a claim to knowledge of the ultimate purpose, we shall clearly perceive that just as one cannot imagine a blossom or seed for any single plant better suited to it than those it produces, so it is impossible to imagine any two people more completely adapted down to the smallest detail for the purpose they had to fulfill, than Napoleon and Alexander with all their antecedents.

CHAPTER III

The fundamental and essential significance of the European events of the beginning of the nineteenth century lies in the movement of the mass of the European peoples from west to east and afterwards from east to west. The commencement of that movement was the movement from west to east. For the peoples of the west to be able to make their warlike movement to Moscow it was necessary: (1) that they should form themselves into a military group of a size able to endure a collision with the warlike military group of the east, (2) that they should abandon all established traditions and customs, and (3) that during their military movement they should have at their head a man who could justify to himself and to them the deceptions, robberies, and murders which would have to be committed during that movement.

And beginning with the French Revolution the old inadequately large group was destroyed, as well as the old habits and traditions, and step by step a group was formed of larger dimensions with new customs and traditions, and a man was produced who would stand at the head of the coming movement and bear the responsibility for all that had to be done.

A man without convictions, without habits, without traditions, without a name, and not even a Frenchman, emerges—by what seem the strangest chances—from among all the seething French parties, and without joining any one of them is borne forward to a prominent position.

The ignorance of his colleagues, the weakness and insignificance of his opponents, the frankness of his falsehoods, and the dazzling and self-confident limitations of this man raise him to the head of the army. The brilliant qualities of the soldiers of the army sent to Italy, his opponents' reluctance to fight, and his own childish audacity and self-confidence secure him military fame. Innumerable so-called *chances* accompany him everywhere. The disfavor into which he falls with the rulers of France turns to his advantage. His attempts to avoid his predestined path are unsuccessful: he is not received into the Russian service, and the appointment he seeks in Turkey comes to nothing. During the war in Italy he is several times on the verge of destruction and each time is saved in an unexpected manner. Owing to various diplomatic considerations the Russian armies—just those which might have destroyed his prestige—do not appear upon the scene till he is no longer there.

On his return from Italy he finds the government in Paris in a process of dissolution in which all those who are in it are inevitably wiped out and destroyed. And by chance an escape from this dangerous position presents itself in the form of an aimless and senseless expedition to Africa. Again so-called *chance* accompanies him. Impregnable Malta surrenders without a shot; his most reckless schemes are crowned with success. The enemy's fleet, which subsequently did not let a single boat pass, allows his entire army to elude it. In Africa a whole series of outrages are committed against the almost unarmed inhabitants. And the men who commit these crimes, especially their leader, assure themselves that this is admirable, this is glory—it resembles Caesar and Alexander the Great and is therefore good.

This ideal of *glory* and *grandeur*—which consists not merely in considering nothing wrong that one does but in priding oneself on every crime one commits, ascribing to it an incomprehensible supernatural significance—that ideal, destined to guide this man and his associates, had scope for its development in Africa. Whatever he does succeeds. The plague does not touch him. The cruelty of murdering prisoners is not imputed to him as a fault. His childishly rash, uncalled-for, and ignoble departure from Africa, leaving his comrades in distress, is set down to his credit, and again the enemy's fleet twice lets him slip past. When, intoxicated by the crimes he has committed so successfully, he reaches Paris, the dissolution of the republican government, which a year earlier might have ruined him, has reached its extreme limit, and his presence there now as a newcomer free from party entanglements can only serve to exalt him—and though he himself has no plan, he is quite ready for his new rôle.

He had no plan, he was afraid of everything, but the parties snatched at him and demanded his participation.

He alone—with his ideal of glory and grandeur developed in Italy and Egypt, his insane self-adulation, his boldness in crime and frankness in lying—he alone could justify what had to be done.

He is needed for the place that awaits him, and so almost apart from his will and despite his indecision, his lack of a plan, and all his mistakes, he is drawn into a conspiracy that aims at seizing power and the conspiracy is crowned with success.

He is pushed into a meeting of the legislature. In alarm he wishes to flee, considering himself lost. He pretends to fall into a swoon and says senseless things that should have ruined him. But the once proud and shrewd rulers of France, feeling that their part is played out, are even more bewildered than he, and do not say the words they should have said to destroy him and retain their power.

Chance, millions of *chances*, give him power, and all men as if by agreement co-operate to confirm that power. *Chance* forms the characters of the rulers of France, who submit to him; *chance* forms the character of Paul I of Russia who recognizes his government; *chance* contrives a plot against him which not only fails to harm him but confirms his power. *Chance* puts the Duc d'Enghien in his hands and unexpectedly causes him to kill him—thereby convincing the mob more forcibly than in any other way that he had the right, since he had the might. *Chance* contrives that though he directs all his efforts to prepare an expedition against England (which would inevitably have ruined him) he never carries out that intention, but unexpectedly falls upon Mack and the Austrians, who surrender without a battle. *Chance* and *genius* give him the victory at Austerlitz; and by *chance* all men, not only the French but all Europe—except England which does not take part in the events about to happen—despite their former horror and detestation of his crimes, now recognize his authority, the title he has given himself, and his ideal of grandeur and glory, which seems excellent and reasonable to them all.

As if measuring themselves and preparing for the coming movement, the western forces push toward the east several times in

1805, 1806, 1807, and 1809, gaining strength and growing. In 1811 the group of people that had formed in France unites into one group with the peoples of Central Europe. The strength of the justification of the man who stands at the head of the movement grows with the increased size of the group. During the ten-year preparatory period this man had formed relations with all the crowned heads of Europe. The discredited rulers of the world can oppose no reasonable ideal to the insensate Napoleonic ideal of *glory* and *grandeur*. One after another they hasten to display their insignificance before him. The King of Prussia sends his wife to seek the great man's mercy; the Emperor of Austria considers it a favor that this man receives a daughter of the Caesars into his bed; the Pope, the guardian of all that the nations hold sacred, utilizes religion for the aggrandizement of the great man. It is not Napoleon who prepares himself for the accomplishment of his role, so much as all those round him who prepare him to take on himself the whole responsibility for what is happening and has to happen. There is no step, no crime or petty fraud he commits, which in the mouths of those around him is not at once represented as a great deed. The most suitable fête the Germans can devise for him is a celebration of Jena and Auerstädt. Not only is he great, but so are his ancestors, his brothers, his stepsons, and his brothers-in-law. Everything is done to deprive him of the remains of his reason and to prepare him for his terrible part. And when he is ready so too are the forces.

The invasion pushes eastward and reaches its final goal— Moscow. That city is taken; the Russian army suffers heavier losses than the opposing armies had suffered in the former war from Austerlitz to Wagram. But suddenly instead of those *chances* and that *genius* which hitherto had so consistently led him by an uninterrupted series of successes to the predestined goal, an innumerable sequence of inverse *chances* occur—from the cold in his head at Borodinó to the sparks which set Moscow on fire, and the frosts—and instead of *genius*, stupidity and immeasurable baseness become evident.

The invaders flee, turn back, flee again, and all the chances are now not for Napoleon but always against him.

A countermovement is then accomplished from east to west with a remarkable resemblance to the preceding movement from west to east. Attempted drives from east to west—similar to the contrary movements of 1805, 1807, and 1809—precede the great westward movement; there is the same coalescence into a group of enormous dimensions; the same adhesion of the people of Central Europe to the movement; the same hesitation midway, and the same increasing rapidity as the goal is approached.

Paris, the ultimate goal, is reached. The Napoleonic government and army are destroyed. Napoleon himself is no longer of any account; all his actions are evidently pitiful and mean, but again an inexplicable *chance* occurs. The allies detest Napoleon whom they regard as the cause of their sufferings. Deprived of power and authority, his crimes and his craft exposed, he should have appeared to them what he appeared ten years previously and one year later— an outlawed brigand. But by some strange chance no one perceives this. His part is not yet ended. The man who ten years before and a year later was considered an outlawed brigand is sent to an island two days' sail from France, which for some reason is presented to him as his dominion, and guards are given to him and millions of money are paid him.

CHAPTER IV

The flood of nations begins to subside into its normal channels. The waves of the great movement abate, and on the calm surface eddies are formed in which float the diplomatists, who imagine that they have caused the floods to abate.

But the smooth sea again suddenly becomes disturbed. The diplomatists think that their disagreements are the cause of this fresh pressure of natural forces; they anticipate war between their sovereigns; the position seems to them insoluble. But the wave they feel to be rising does not come from the quarter they expect. It rises again from the same point as before—Paris. The last backwash of the movement from the west occurs: a backwash which serves to solve the apparently insuperable diplomatic difficulties and ends the military movement of that period of history.

The man who had devastated France returns to France alone, without any conspiracy and without soldiers. Any guard might arrest him, but by strange chance no one does so and all rapturously greet the man they cursed the day before and will curse again a month later.

This man is still needed to justify the final collective act.

That act is performed.

The last rôle is played. The actor is bidden to disrobe and wash off his powder and paint: he will not be wanted any more.

And some years pass during which he plays a pitiful comedy to himself in solitude on his island, justifying his actions by intrigues and lies when the justification is no longer needed, and displaying to the whole world what it was that people had mistaken for strength as long as an unseen hand directed his actions.

The manager having brought the drama to a close and stripped the actor shows him to us.

"See what you believed in! This is he! Do you now see that it was not he but I who moved you?"

But dazed by the force of the movement, it was long before people understood this.

Still greater coherence and inevitability is seen in the life of Alexander I, the man who stood at the head of the countermovement from east to west.

What was needed for him who, overshadowing others, stood at the head of that movement from east to west?

What was needed was a sense of justice and a sympathy with European affairs, but a remote sympathy not dulled by petty interests; a moral superiority over those sovereigns of the day who co-operated with him; a mild and attractive personality; and a personal grievance against Napoleon. And all this was found in Alexander I; all this had been prepared by innumerable so-called *chances* in his life: his education, his early liberalism, the advisers who surrounded him, and by Austerlitz, and Tilsit, and Erfurt.

During the national war he was inactive because he was not needed. But as soon as the necessity for a general European war presented itself he appeared in his place at the given moment and, uniting the nations of Europe, led them to the goal.

The goal is reached. After the final war of 1815 Alexander possesses all possible power. How does he use it?

Alexander I—the pacifier of Europe, the man who from his early years had striven only for his people's welfare, the originator of the liberal innovations in his fatherland—now that he seemed to possess the utmost power and therefore to have the possibility of bringing about the welfare of his peoples—at the time when Napoleon in exile was drawing up childish and mendacious plans of how he would have made mankind happy had he retained power—Alexander I, having fulfilled his mission and feeling the hand of God upon him, suddenly recognizes the insignificance of that supposed power, turns away from it, and gives it into the hands of contemptible men whom he despises, saying only:

"Not unto us, not unto us, but unto Thy Name!... I too am a man like the rest of you. Let me live like a man and think of my soul and of God."

As the sun and each atom of ether is a sphere complete in itself, and yet at the same time only a part of a whole too immense for man to comprehend, so each individual has within himself his own aims and yet has them to serve a general purpose incomprehensible to man.

A bee settling on a flower has stung a child. And the child is afraid of bees and declares that bees exist to sting people. A poet admires the bee sucking from the chalice of a flower and says it exists to suck the fragrance of flowers. A beekeeper, seeing the bee collect pollen from flowers and carry it to the hive, says that it exists to gather honey. Another beekeeper who has studied the life of the hive more closely says that the bee gathers pollen dust to feed the young bees and rear a queen, and that it exists to perpetuate its race. A botanist notices that the bee flying with the pollen of a male flower to a pistil fertilizes the latter, and sees in this the purpose of the bee's existence. Another, observing the migration of plants, notices that the bee helps in this work, and may say that in this lies the purpose of the bee. But the ultimate purpose of the bee is not exhausted by the first, the second, or any of the processes the human mind can discern. The higher the human intellect rises in the discovery of these purposes, the more obvious it becomes, that the ultimate purpose is beyond our comprehension.

All that is accessible to man is the relation of the life of the bee to other manifestations of life. And so it is with the purpose of historic characters and nations.

CHAPTER V

Natásha's wedding to Bezúkhov, which took place in 1813, was the last happy event in the family of the old Rostóvs. Count IlyáRostóv died that same year and, as always happens, after the father's death the family group broke up.

The events of the previous year: the burning of Moscow and the flight from it, the death of Prince Andrew, Natásha's despair, Pétya's death, and the old countess' grief fell blow after blow on the old count's head. He seemed to be unable to understand the meaning of all these events, and bowed his old head in a spiritual sense as if expecting and inviting further blows which would finish him. He seemed now frightened and distraught and now unnaturally animated and enterprising.

The arrangements for Natásha's marriage occupied him for a while. He ordered dinners and suppers and obviously tried to appear cheerful, but his cheerfulness was not infectious as it used to be: on the contrary it evoked the compassion of those who knew and liked him.

When Pierre and his wife had left, he grew very quiet and began to complain of depression. A few days later he fell ill and took to his bed. He realized from the first that he would not get up again, despite the doctor's encouragement. The countess passed a fortnight in an armchair by his pillow without undressing. Every time she gave him his medicine he sobbed and silently kissed her hand. On his last day, sobbing, he asked her and his absent son to forgive him for having dissipated their property—that being the chief fault of which he was conscious. After receiving communion and unction he quietly died; and next day a throng of acquaintances who came to pay their last respects to the deceased filled the house rented by the Rostóvs. All these acquaintances, who had so often dined and danced at his house and had so often laughed at him, now said, with a common feeling of self-reproach and emotion, as if justifying themselves: "Well, whatever he may have been he was a most worthy man. You don't meet such men nowadays.... And which of us has not weaknesses of his own?"

It was just when the count's affairs had become so involved that it was impossible to say what would happen if he lived another year that he unexpectedly died.

Nicholas was with the Russian army in Paris when the news of his father's death reached him. He at once resigned his commission, and without waiting for it to be accepted took leave of absence and went to Moscow. The state of the count's affairs became quite obvious a month after his death, surprising everyone by the immense total of small debts the existence of which no one had suspected. The debts amounted to double the value of the property.

Friends and relations advised Nicholas to decline the inheritance. But he regarded such a refusal as a slur on his father's memory, which he held sacred, and therefore would not hear of refusing and accepted the inheritance together with the obligation to pay the debts.

The creditors who had so long been silent, restrained by a vague but powerful influence exerted on them while he lived by the count's careless good nature, all proceeded to enforce their claims at once. As always happens in such cases rivalry sprang up as to which should get paid first, and those who like Mítenka held promissory notes given them as presents now became the most exacting of the creditors. Nicholas was allowed no respite and no peace, and those who had seemed to pity the old man—the cause of their losses (if they were losses)—now remorselessly pursued the young heir who had voluntarily undertaken the debts and was obviously not guilty of contracting them.

Not one of the plans Nicholas tried succeeded; the estate was sold by auction for half its value, and half the debts still remained unpaid. Nicholas accepted thirty thousand rubles offered him by his brother-in-law Bezúkhov to pay off debts he regarded as genuinely due for value received. And to avoid being imprisoned for the remainder, as the creditors threatened, he re-entered the government service.

He could not rejoin the army where he would have been made colonel at the next vacancy, for his mother now clung to him as her one hold on life; and so despite his reluctance to remain in Moscow among people who had known him before, and despite his abhorrence of the civil service, he accepted a post in Moscow in that service, doffed the uniform of which he was so fond, and moved with his mother and Sónya to a small house on the SívtsevVrazhók.

Natásha and Pierre were living in Petersburg at the time and had no clear idea of Nicholas' circumstances. Having borrowed money from his brother-in-law, Nicholas tried to hide his wretched condition from him. His position was the more difficult because with his salary of twelve hundred rubles he had not only to keep himself, his mother, and Sónya, but had to shield his mother from knowledge of their poverty. The countess could not conceive of life without the luxurious conditions she had been used to from childhood and, unable to realize how hard it was for her son, kept demanding now a carriage (which they did not keep) to send for a friend, now some expensive article of food for herself, or wine for her son, or money to buy a present as a surprise for Natásha or Sónya, or for Nicholas himself.

Sónya kept house, attended on her aunt, read to her, put up with her whims and secret ill-will, and helped Nicholas to conceal their poverty from the old countess. Nicholas felt himself irredeemably indebted to Sónya for all she was doing for his mother and greatly admired her patience and devotion, but tried to keep aloof from her.

He seemed in his heart to reproach her for being too perfect, and because there was nothing to reproach her with. She had all that people are valued for, but little that could have made him love her. He felt that the more he valued her the less he loved her. He had taken her at her word when she wrote giving him his freedom and now behaved as if all that had passed between them had been long forgotten and could never in any case be renewed.

Nicholas' position became worse and worse. The idea of putting something aside out of his salary proved a dream. Not only did he not save anything, but to comply with his mother's demands he even incurred some small debts. He could see no way out of this situation. The idea of marrying some rich woman, which was suggested to him by his female relations, was repugnant to him. The other way out—his mother's death—never entered his head. He wished for nothing and hoped for nothing, and deep in his heart experienced a gloomy and stern satisfaction in an uncomplaining endurance of his position. He tried to avoid his old acquaintances with their commiseration and offensive offers of assistance; he avoided all distraction and recreation, and even at home did nothing but play cards with his mother, pace silently up and down the room, and smoke one pipe after another. He seemed carefully to cherish within himself the gloomy mood which alone enabled him to endure his position.

CHAPTER VI

At the beginning of winter Princess Mary came to Moscow. From reports current in town she learned how the Rostóvs were situated, and how "the son has sacrificed himself for his mother," as people were saying.

"I never expected anything else of him," said Princess Mary to herself, feeling a joyous sense of her love for him. Remembering her friendly relations with all the Rostóvs which had made her almost a member of the family, she thought it her duty to go to see them. But remembering her relations with Nicholas in Vorónezh she was shy about doing so. Making a great effort she did however go to call on them a few weeks after her arrival in Moscow.

Nicholas was the first to meet her, as the countess' room could only be reached through his. But instead of being greeted with pleasure as she had expected, at his first glance at her his face assumed a cold, stiff, proud expression she had not seen on it before. He inquired about her health, led the way to his mother, and having sat there for five minutes left the room.

When the princess came out of the countess' room Nicholas met her again, and with marked solemnity and stiffness accompanied her to the anteroom. To her remarks about his mother's health he made no reply. "What's that to you? Leave me in peace," his looks seemed to say.

"Why does she come prowling here? What does she want? I can't bear these ladies and all these civilities!" said he aloud in Sónya's presence, evidently unable to repress his vexation, after the princess' carriage had disappeared.

"Oh, Nicholas, how can you talk like that?" cried Sónya, hardly able to conceal her delight. "She is so kind and Mamma is so fond of her!"

Nicholas did not reply and tried to avoid speaking of the princess any more. But after her visit the old countess spoke of her several times a day.

She sang her praises, insisted that her son must call on her, expressed a wish to see her often, but yet always became ill-humored when she began to talk about her.

Nicholas tried to keep silence when his mother spoke of the princess, but his silence irritated her.

"She is a very admirable and excellent young woman," said she, "and you must go and call on her. You would at least be seeing somebody, and I think it must be dull for you only seeing us."

"But I don't in the least want to, Mamma."

"You used to want to, and now you don't. Really I don't understand you, my dear. One day you are dull, and the next you refuse to see anyone."

"But I never said I was dull."

"Why, you said yourself you don't want even to see her. She is a very admirable young woman and you always liked her, but now suddenly you have got some notion or other in your head. You hide everything from me."

"Not at all, Mamma."

"If I were asking you to do something disagreeable now—but I only ask you to return a call. One would think mere politeness required it.... Well, I have asked you, and now I won't interfere any more since you have secrets from your mother."

"Well, then, I'll go if you wish it."

"It doesn't matter to me. I only wish it for your sake."

Nicholas sighed, bit his mustache, and laid out the cards for a patience, trying to divert his mother's attention to another topic.

The same conversation was repeated next day and the day after, and the day after that.

After her visit to the Rostóvs and her unexpectedly chilly reception by Nicholas, Princess Mary confessed to herself that she had been right in not wishing to be the first to call.

"I expected nothing else," she told herself, calling her pride to her aid. "I have nothing to do with him and I only wanted to see the old lady, who was always kind to me and to whom I am under many obligations."

But she could not pacify herself with these reflections; a feeling akin to remorse troubled her when she thought of her visit. Though she had firmly resolved not to call on the Rostóvs again and to forget the whole matter, she felt herself all the time in an awkward position. And when she asked herself what distressed her, she had to admit that it was her relation to Rostóv. His cold, polite manner did not express his feeling for her (she knew that) but it concealed something, and until she could discover what that something was, she felt that she could not be at ease.

One day in midwinter when sitting in the schoolroom attending to her nephew's lessons, she was informed that Rostóv had called. With a firm resolution not to betray herself and not show her agitation, she sent for Mademoiselle Bourienne and went with her to the drawing room.

Her first glance at Nicholas' face told her that he had only come to fulfill the demands of politeness, and she firmly resolved to maintain the tone in which he addressed her.

They spoke of the countess' health, of their mutual friends, of the latest war news, and when the ten minutes required by propriety had elapsed after which a visitor may rise, Nicholas got up to say good-by.

With Mademoiselle Bourienne's help the princess had maintained the conversation very well, but at the very last moment, just when he rose, she was so tired of talking of what did not interest her, and her mind was so full of the question why she alone was granted so little happiness in life, that in a fit of absent-mindedness she sat still, her luminous eyes gazing fixedly before her, not noticing that he had risen.

Nicholas glanced at her and, wishing to appear not to notice her abstraction, made some remark to Mademoiselle Bourienne and then again looked at the princess. She still sat motionless with a look of suffering on her gentle face. He suddenly felt sorry for her and was vaguely conscious that he might be the cause of the sadness her face expressed. He wished to help her and say something pleasant, but could think of nothing to say.

"Good-by, Princess!" said he.

She started, flushed, and sighed deeply.

"Oh, I beg your pardon," she said as if waking up. "Are you going already, Count? Well then, good-by! Oh, but the cushion for the countess!"

"Wait a moment, I'll fetch it," said Mademoiselle Bourienne, and she left the room.

They both sat silent, with an occasional glance at one another.

"Yes, Princess," said Nicholas at last with a sad smile, "it doesn't seem long ago since we first met at Boguchárovo, but how much water has flowed since then! In what distress we all seemed to be then, yet I would give much to bring back that time... but there's no bringing it back."

Princess Mary gazed intently into his eyes with her own luminous ones as he said this. She seemed to be trying to fathom the hidden meaning of his words which would explain his feeling for her.

"Yes, yes," said she, "but you have no reason to regret the past, Count. As I understand your present life, I think you will always recall it with satisfaction, because the self-sacrifice that fills it now..."

"I cannot accept your praise," he interrupted her hurriedly. "On the contrary I continually reproach myself.... But this is not at all an interesting or cheerful subject."

His face again resumed its former stiff and cold expression. But the princess had caught a glimpse of the man she had known and loved, and it was to him that she now spoke.

"I thought you would allow me to tell you this," she said. "I had come so near to you... and to all your family that I thought you would not consider my sympathy misplaced, but I was mistaken," and suddenly her voice trembled. "I don't know why," she continued, recovering herself, "but you used to be different, and..."

"There are a thousand reasons *why*," laying special emphasis on the *why*. "Thank you, Princess," he added softly. "Sometimes it is hard."

"So that's why! That's why!" a voice whispered in Princess Mary's soul. "No, it was not only that gay, kind, and frank look, not only that handsome exterior, that I loved in him. I divined his noble, resolute, self-sacrificing spirit too," she said to herself. "Yes, he is poor now and I am rich.... Yes, that's the only reason.... Yes, were it not for that..." And remembering his former tenderness, and looking now at his kind, sorrowful face, she suddenly understood the cause of his coldness.

"But why, Count, why?" she almost cried, unconsciously moving closer to him. "Why? Tell me. You must tell me!"

He was silent.

"I don't understand your *why*, Count," she continued, "but it's hard for me... I confess it. For some reason you wish to deprive me of our former friendship. And that hurts me." There were tears in her eyes and in her voice. "I have had so little happiness in life that every loss is hard for me to bear.... Excuse me, good-by!" and suddenly she began to cry and was hurrying from the room.

"Princess, for God's sake!" he exclaimed, trying to stop her. "Princess!"

She turned round. For a few seconds they gazed silently into one another's eyes—and what had seemed impossible and remote suddenly became possible, inevitable, and very near.

CHAPTER VII

In the winter of 1813 Nicholas married Princess Mary and moved to Bald Hills with his wife, his mother, and Sónya.

Within four years he had paid off all his remaining debts without selling any of his wife's property, and having received a small inheritance on the death of a cousin he paid his debt to Pierre as well.

In another three years, by 1820, he had so managed his affairs that he was able to buy a small estate adjoining Bald Hills and was negotiating to buy back Otrádnoe—that being his pet dream.

Having started farming from necessity, he soon grew so devoted to it that it became his favorite and almost his sole occupation. Nicholas was a plain farmer: he did not like innovations, especially the English ones then coming into vogue. He laughed at theoretical treatises on estate management, disliked factories, the raising of expensive products, and the buying of expensive seed corn, and did not make a hobby of any particular part of the work on his estate. He always had before his mind's eye *the estate* as a whole and not any particular part of it. The chief thing in his eyes was not the nitrogen in the soil, nor the oxygen in the air, nor manures, nor special plows, but that most important agent by which nitrogen, oxygen, manure, and plow were made effective—the peasant laborer. When Nicholas first began farming and began to understand its different branches, it was the serf who especially attracted his attention. The peasant seemed to him not merely a tool, but also a judge of farming and an end in himself. At first he watched the serfs, trying to understand their aims and what they considered good and bad, and only pretended to direct them and give orders while in reality learning from them their methods, their manner of speech, and their judgment of what was good and bad. Only when he had understood the peasants' tastes and aspirations, had learned to talk their language, to grasp the hidden meaning of their words, and felt akin to them did he begin boldly to manage his serfs, that is, to perform toward them the duties demanded of him. And Nicholas' management produced very brilliant results.

Guided by some gift of insight, on taking up the management of the estates he at once unerringly appointed as bailiff, village elder, and delegate, the very men the serfs would themselves have chosen had they had the right to choose, and these posts never changed hands. Before analyzing the properties of manure, before entering into the *debit* and *credit* (as he ironically called it), he found out how many cattle the peasants had and increased the number by all possible means. He kept the peasant families together in the largest groups possible, not allowing the family groups to divide into separate households. He was hard alike on the lazy, the depraved, and the weak, and tried to get them expelled from the commune.

He was as careful of the sowing and reaping of the peasants' hay and corn as of his own, and few landowners had their crops sown and harvested so early and so well, or got so good a return, as did Nicholas.

He disliked having anything to do with the domestic serfs—the "drones" as he called them—and everyone said he spoiled them by his laxity. When a decision had to be taken regarding a domestic serf, especially if one had to be punished, he always felt undecided and consulted everybody in the house; but when it was possible to have a domestic serf conscripted instead of a land worker he did so without the least hesitation. He never felt any hesitation in dealing with the peasants. He knew that his every decision would be approved by them all with very few exceptions.

He did not allow himself either to be hard on or punish a man, or to make things easy for or reward anyone, merely because he felt inclined to do so. He could not have said by what standard he judged what he should or should not do, but the standard was quite firm and definite in his own mind.

Often, speaking with vexation of some failure or irregularity, he would say: "What can one do with our Russian peasants?" and imagined that he could not bear them.

Yet he loved "our Russian peasants" and their way of life with his whole soul, and for that very reason had understood and assimilated the one way and manner of farming which produced good results.

Countess Mary was jealous of this passion of her husband's and regretted that she could not share it; but she could not understand the joys and vexations he derived from that world, to her so remote and alien. She could not understand why he was so particularly animated and happy when, after getting up at daybreak and spending the whole morning in the fields or on the threshing floor, he returned from the sowing or mowing or reaping to have tea with her. She did not understand why he spoke with such admiration and delight of the farming of the thrifty and well-to-do peasant Matthew Ermíshin, who with his family had carted corn all night; or of the fact that his (Nicholas') sheaves were already stacked before anyone else had his harvest in. She did not understand why he stepped out from the window to the veranda and smiled under his mustache and winked so joyfully, when warm steady rain began to fall on the dry and thirsty shoots of the young oats, or why when the wind carried away a threatening cloud during the hay harvest he would return from the barn, flushed, sunburned, and perspiring, with a smell of wormwood and gentian in his hair and, gleefully rubbing his hands, would say: "Well, one more day and my grain and the peasants' will all be under cover."

Still less did she understand why he, kindhearted and always ready to anticipate her wishes, should become almost desperate when she brought him a petition from some peasant men or women who had appealed to her to be excused some work; why he, that kind Nicholas, should obstinately refuse her, angrily asking her not to interfere in what was not her business. She felt he had a world apart, which he loved passionately and which had laws she had not fathomed.

Sometimes when, trying to understand him, she spoke of the good work he was doing for his serfs, he would be vexed and reply: "Not in the least; it never entered my head and I wouldn't do *that* for their good! That's all poetry and old wives' talk—all that doing good to one's neighbor! What I want is that our children should not have to go begging. I must put our affairs in order while I am alive, that's all. And to do that, order and strictness are essential.... That's all about it!" said he, clenching his vigorous fist. "And fairness, of course," he added, "for if the peasant is naked and hungry and has only one miserable horse, he can do no good either for himself or for me."

And all Nicholas did was fruitful—probably just because he refused to allow himself to think that he was doing good to others for virtue's sake. His means increased rapidly; serfs from neighboring estates came to beg him to buy them, and long after his death the memory of his administration was devoutly preserved among the serfs. "He was a master... the peasants' affairs first and then his own. Of course he was not to be trifled with either—in a word, he was a real master!"

CHAPTER VIII

One matter connected with his management sometimes worried Nicholas, and that was his quick temper together with his old hussar habit of making free use of his fists. At first he saw nothing reprehensible in this, but in the second year of his marriage his view of that form of punishment suddenly changed.

Once in summer he had sent for the village elder from Boguchárovo, a man who had succeeded to the post when Dron died and who was accused of dishonesty and various irregularities. Nicholas went out into the porch to question him, and immediately after the elder had given a few replies the sound of cries and blows were heard. On returning to lunch Nicholas went up to his wife, who sat with her head bent low over her embroidery frame, and as usual began to tell her what he had been doing that morning. Among other things he spoke of the Boguchárovo elder. Countess Mary turned red and then pale, but continued to sit with head bowed and lips compressed and gave her husband no reply.

"Such an insolent scoundrel!" he cried, growing hot again at the mere recollection of him. "If he had told me he was drunk and did not see... But what is the matter with you, Mary?" he suddenly asked.

Countess Mary raised her head and tried to speak, but hastily looked down again and her lips puckered.

"Why, whatever is the matter, my dearest?"

The looks of the plain Countess Mary always improved when she was in tears. She never cried from pain or vexation, but always from sorrow or pity, and when she wept her radiant eyes acquired an irresistible charm.

The moment Nicholas took her hand she could no longer restrain herself and began to cry.

"Nicholas, I saw it... he was to blame, but why do you... Nicholas!" and she covered her face with her hands.

Nicholas said nothing. He flushed crimson, left her side, and paced up and down the room. He understood what she was weeping about, but could not in his heart at once agree with her that what he had regarded from childhood as quite an everyday event was wrong. "Is it just sentimentality, old wives' tales, or is she right?" he asked himself. Before he had solved that point he glanced again at her face filled with love and pain, and he suddenly realized that she was right and that he had long been sinning against himself.

"Mary," he said softly, going up to her, "it will never happen again; I give you my word. Never," he repeated in a trembling voice like a boy asking for forgiveness.

The tears flowed faster still from the countess' eyes. She took his hand and kissed it.

"Nicholas, when did you break your cameo?" she asked to change the subject, looking at his finger on which he wore a ring with a cameo of Laocoön's head.

"Today—it was the same affair. Oh, Mary, don't remind me of it!" and again he flushed. "I give you my word of honor it shan't occur again, and let this always be a reminder to me," and he pointed to the broken ring.

After that, when in discussions with his village elders or stewards the blood rushed to his face and his fists began to clench, Nicholas would turn the broken ring on his finger and would drop his eyes before the man who was making him angry. But he did forget himself once or twice within a twelvemonth, and then he would go and confess to his wife, and would again promise that this should really be the very last time.

"Mary, you must despise me!" he would say. "I deserve it."

"You should go, go away at once, if you don't feel strong enough to control yourself," she would reply sadly, trying to comfort her husband.

Among the gentry of the province Nicholas was respected but not liked. He did not concern himself with the interests of his own class, and consequently some thought him proud and others thought him stupid. The whole summer, from spring sowing to harvest, he was busy with the work on his farm. In autumn he gave himself up to hunting with the same business-like seriousness—leaving home for a month, or even two, with his hunt. In winter he visited his other villages or spent his time reading. The books he read were chiefly historical, and on these he spent a certain sum every year. He was collecting, as he said, a serious library, and he made it a rule to read through all the books he bought. He would sit in his study with a grave air, reading—a task he first imposed upon himself as a duty, but which afterwards became a habit affording him a special kind of pleasure and a consciousness of being occupied with serious matters. In winter, except for business excursions, he spent most of his time at home making himself one with his family and entering into all the details of his children's relations with their mother. The harmony between him and his wife grew closer and closer and he daily discovered fresh spiritual treasures in her.

From the time of his marriage Sónya had lived in his house. Before that, Nicholas had told his wife all that had passed between himself and Sónya, blaming himself and commending her. He had asked Princess Mary to be gentle and kind to his cousin. She thoroughly realized the wrong he had done Sónya, felt herself to blame toward her, and imagined that her wealth had influenced Nicholas' choice. She could not find fault with Sónya in any way and tried to be fond of her, but often felt ill-will toward her which she could not overcome.

Once she had a talk with her friend Natásha about Sónya and about her own injustice toward her.

"You know," said Natásha, "you have read the Gospels a great deal—there is a passage in them that just fits Sónya."

"What?" asked Countess Mary, surprised.

"'To him that hath shall be given, and from him that hath not shall be taken away.' You remember? She is one that hath not; why, I don't know. Perhaps she lacks egotism, I don't know, but from her is taken away, and everything has been taken away. Sometimes I am dreadfully sorry for her. Formerly I very much wanted Nicholas to marry her, but I always had a sort of presentiment that it would not come off. She is a *sterile flower*, you know—like some strawberry blossoms. Sometimes I am sorry for her, and sometimes I think she doesn't feel it as you or I would."

Though Countess Mary told Natásha that those words in the Gospel must be understood differently, yet looking at Sónya she agreed with Natásha's explanation. It really seemed that Sónya did not feel her position trying, and had grown quite reconciled to her lot as a *sterile flower*. She seemed to be fond not so much of individuals as of the family as a whole. Like a cat, she had attached herself not to the people but to the home. She waited on the old countess, petted and spoiled the children, was always ready to render the small services for which she had a gift, and all this was unconsciously accepted from her with insufficient gratitude.

The country seat at Bald Hills had been rebuilt, though not on the same scale as under the old prince.

The buildings, begun under straitened circumstances, were more than simple. The immense house on the old stone foundations was of wood, plastered only inside. It had bare deal floors and was furnished with very simple hard sofas, armchairs, tables, and chairs made by their own serf carpenters out of their own birchwood. The house was spacious and had rooms for the house serfs and apartments for visitors. Whole families of the Rostóvs' and Bolkónskis' relations sometimes came to Bald Hills with sixteen horses and dozens of servants and stayed for months. Besides that, four times a year, on the name days and birthdays of the hosts, as many as a hundred visitors would gather there for a day or two. The rest of the year life pursued its unbroken routine with its ordinary occupations, and its breakfasts, lunches, dinners, and suppers, provided out of the produce of the estate.

CHAPTER IX

It was the eve of St. Nicholas, the fifth of December, 1820. Natásha had been staying at her brother's with her husband and children since early autumn. Pierre had gone to Petersburg on business of his own for three weeks as he said, but had remained there nearly seven weeks and was expected back every minute.

Besides the Bezúkhov family, Nicholas' old friend the retired General VasíliDmítrichDenísov was staying with the Rostóvs this fifth of December.

On the sixth, which was his name day when the house would be full of visitors, Nicholas knew he would have to exchange his Tartar tunic for a tail coat, and put on narrow boots with pointed toes, and drive to the new church he had built, and then receive visitors who would come to congratulate him, offer them refreshments, and talk about the elections of the nobility; but he considered himself entitled to spend the eve of that day in his usual way. He examined the bailiff's accounts of the village in Ryazán which belonged to his wife's nephew, wrote two business letters, and walked over to the granaries, cattle yards and stables before dinner. Having taken precautions against the general drunkenness to be expected on the morrow because it was a great saint's day, he returned to dinner, and without having time for a private talk with his wife sat down at the long table laid for twenty persons, at which the whole household had assembled. At that table were his mother, his mother's old lady companion Belóva, his wife, their three children with their governess and tutor, his wife's nephew with his tutor, Sónya, Denísov, Natásha, her three children, their governess, and old Michael Ivánovich, the late prince's architect, who was living on in retirement at Bald Hills.

Countess Mary sat at the other end of the table. When her husband took his place she concluded, from the rapid manner in which after taking up his table napkin he pushed back the tumbler and wineglass standing before him, that he was out of humor, as was sometimes the case when he came in to dinner straight from the farm—especially before the soup. Countess Mary well knew that mood of his, and when she herself was in a good frame of mind quietly waited till he had had his soup and then began to talk to him and make him admit that there was no cause for his ill-humor. But today she quite forgot that and was hurt that he should be angry with her without any reason, and she felt unhappy. She asked him where he had been. He replied. She again inquired whether everything was going well on the farm. Her unnatural tone made him wince unpleasantly and he replied hastily.

"Then I'm not mistaken," thought Countess Mary. "Why is he cross with me?" She concluded from his tone that he was vexed with her and wished to end the conversation. She knew her remarks sounded unnatural, but could not refrain from asking some more questions.

Thanks to Denísov the conversation at table soon became general and lively, and she did not talk to her husband. When they left the table and went as usual to thank the old countess, Countess Mary held out her hand and kissed her husband, and asked him why he was angry with her.

"You always have such strange fancies! I didn't even think of being angry," he replied.

But the word *always* seemed to her to imply: "Yes, I am angry but I won't tell you why."

Nicholas and his wife lived together so happily that even Sónya and the old countess, who felt jealous and would have liked them to disagree, could find nothing to reproach them with; but even they had their moments of antagonism. Occasionally, and it was always just after they had been happiest together, they suddenly had a feeling of estrangement and hostility, which occurred most frequently during Countess Mary's pregnancies, and this was such a time.

"Well, *messieurs et mesdames*," said Nicholas loudly and with apparent cheerfulness (it seemed to Countess Mary that he did it on purpose to vex her), "I have been on my feet since six this morning. Tomorrow I shall have to suffer, so today I'll go and rest."

And without a word to his wife he went to the little sitting room and lay down on the sofa.

"That's always the way," thought Countess Mary. "He talks to everyone except me. I see... I see that I am repulsive to him, especially when I am in this condition." She looked down at her expanded figure and in the glass at her pale, sallow, emaciated face in which her eyes now looked larger than ever.

And everything annoyed her—Denísov's shouting and laughter, Natásha's talk, and especially a quick glance Sónya gave her.

Sónya was always the first excuse Countess Mary found for feeling irritated.

Having sat awhile with her visitors without understanding anything of what they were saying, she softly left the room and went to the nursery.

The children were playing at "going to Moscow" in a carriage made of chairs and invited her to go with them. She sat down and played with them a little, but the thought of her husband and his unreasonable crossness worried her. She got up and, walking on tiptoe with difficulty, went to the small sitting room.

"Perhaps he is not asleep; I'll have an explanation with him," she said to herself. Little Andrew, her eldest boy, imitating his mother, followed her on tiptoe. She did not notice him.

"Mary, dear, I think he is asleep—he was so tired," said Sónya, meeting her in the large sitting room (it seemed to Countess Mary that she crossed her path everywhere). "Andrew may wake him."

Countess Mary looked round, saw little Andrew following her, felt that Sónya was right, and for that very reason flushed and with evident difficulty refrained from saying something harsh. She made no reply, but to avoid obeying Sónya beckoned to Andrew to follow her quietly and went to the door. Sónya went away by another door. From the room in which Nicholas was sleeping came the sound of his even breathing, every slightest tone of which was familiar to his wife. As she listened to it she saw before her his smooth handsome forehead, his mustache, and his whole face, as she had so often seen it in the stillness of the night when he slept. Nicholas suddenly moved and cleared his throat. And at that moment little Andrew shouted from outside the door: "Papa! Mamma's standing here!" Countess Mary turned pale with fright and made signs to the boy. He grew silent, and quiet ensued for a moment, terrible to Countess Mary. She knew how Nicholas disliked being waked. Then through the door she heard Nicholas clearing his throat again and stirring, and his voice said crossly:

"I can't get a moment's peace.... Mary, is that you? Why did you bring him here?"

"I only came in to look and did not notice... forgive me...."

Nicholas coughed and said no more. Countess Mary moved away from the door and took the boy back to the nursery. Five minutes later little black-eyed three-year-old Natásha, her father's pet, having learned from her brother that Papa was asleep and Mamma was in the sitting room, ran to her father unobserved by her mother. The dark-eyed little girl boldly opened the creaking door, went up to the sofa with energetic steps of her sturdy little legs, and having examined the position of her father, who was asleep with his back to her, rose on tiptoe and kissed the hand which lay under his head. Nicholas turned with a tender smile on his face.

"Natásha, Natásha!" came Countess Mary's frightened whisper from the door. "Papa wants to sleep."

"No, Mamma, he doesn't want to sleep," said little Natásha with conviction. "He's laughing."

Nicholas lowered his legs, rose, and took his daughter in his arms.

"Come in, Mary," he said to his wife.

She went in and sat down by her husband.

"I did not notice him following me," she said timidly. "I just looked in."

Holding his little girl with one arm, Nicholas glanced at his wife and, seeing her guilty expression, put his other arm around her and kissed her hair.

"May I kiss Mamma?" he asked Natásha.

Natásha smiled bashfully.

"Again!" she commanded, pointing with a peremptory gesture to the spot where Nicholas had placed the kiss.

"I don't know why you think I am cross," said Nicholas, replying to the question he knew was in his wife's mind.

"You have no idea how unhappy, how lonely, I feel when you are like that. It always seems to me..."

"Mary, don't talk nonsense. You ought to be ashamed of yourself!" he said gaily.

"It seems to be that you can't love me, that I am so plain... always... and now... in this cond..."

"Oh, how absurd you are! It is not beauty that endears, it's love that makes us see beauty. It is only Malvínas and women of that kind who are loved for their beauty. But do I love my wife? I don't love her, but... I don't know how to put it. Without you, or when something comes between us like this, I seem lost and can't do anything. Now do I love my finger? I don't love it, but just try to cut it off!"

"I'm not like that myself, but I understand. So you're not angry with me?"

"Awfully angry!" he said, smiling and getting up. And smoothing his hair he began to pace the room.

"Do you know, Mary, what I've been thinking?" he began, immediately thinking aloud in his wife's presence now that they had made it up.

He did not ask if she was ready to listen to him. He did not care. A thought had occurred to him and so it belonged to her also. And he told her of his intention to persuade Pierre to stay with them till spring.

Countess Mary listened till he had finished, made some remark, and in her turn began thinking aloud. Her thoughts were about the children.

"You can see the woman in her already," she said in French, pointing to little Natásha. "You reproach us women with being illogical. Here is our logic. I say: 'Papa wants to sleep!' but she says, 'No, he's laughing.' And she was right," said Countess Mary with a happy smile.

"Yes, yes." And Nicholas, taking his little daughter in his strong hand, lifted her high, placed her on his shoulder, held her by the legs, and paced the room with her. There was an expression of carefree happiness on the faces of both father and daughter.

"But you know you may be unfair. You are too fond of this one," his wife whispered in French.

"Yes, but what am I to do?... I try not to show..."

At that moment they heard the sound of the door pulley and footsteps in the hall and anteroom, as if someone had arrived.

"Somebody has come."

"I am sure it is Pierre. I will go and see," said Countess Mary and left the room.

In her absence Nicholas allowed himself to give his little daughter a gallop round the room. Out of breath, he took the laughing child quickly from his shoulder and pressed her to his heart. His capers reminded him of dancing, and looking at the child's round happy little face he thought of what she would be like when he was an old man, taking her into society and dancing the mazurka with her as his old father had danced *Daniel Cooper* with his daughter.

"It is he, it is he, Nicholas!" said Countess Mary, re-entering the room a few minutes later. "Now our Natásha has come to life. You should have seen her ecstasy, and how he caught it for having stayed away so long. Well, come along now, quick, quick! It's time you two were parted," she added, looking smilingly at the little girl who clung to her father.

Nicholas went out holding the child by the hand.

Countess Mary remained in the sitting room.

"I should never, never have believed that one could be so happy," she whispered to herself. A smile lit up her face but at the same time she sighed, and her deep eyes expressed a quiet sadness as though she felt, through her happiness, that there is another sort of happiness unattainable in this life and of which she involuntarily thought at that instant.

CHAPTER X

Natásha had married in the early spring of 1813, and in 1820 already had three daughters besides a son for whom she had longed and whom she was now nursing. She had grown stouter and broader, so that it was difficult to recognize in this robust, motherly woman the slim, lively Natásha of former days. Her features were more defined and had a calm, soft, and serene expression. In her face there was none of the ever-glowing animation that had formerly burned there and constituted its charm. Now her face and body were often all that one saw, and her soul was not visible at all. All that struck the eye was a strong, handsome, and fertile woman. The old fire very rarely kindled in her face now. That happened only when, as was the case that day, her husband returned home, or a sick child was convalescent, or when she and Countess Mary spoke of Prince Andrew (she never mentioned him to her husband, who she imagined was jealous of Prince Andrew's memory), or on the rare occasions when something happened to induce her to sing, a practice she had quite abandoned since her marriage. At the rare moments when the old fire did kindle in her handsome, fully developed body she was even more attractive than in former days.

Since their marriage Natásha and her husband had lived in Moscow, in Petersburg, on their estate near Moscow, or with her mother, that is to say, in Nicholas' house. The young Countess Bezúkhova was not often seen in society, and those who met her there were not pleased with her and found her neither attractive nor amiable. Not that Natásha liked solitude—she did not know whether she liked it or not, she even thought that she did not—but with her pregnancies, her confinements, the nursing of her children, and sharing every moment of her husband's life, she had demands on her time which could be satisfied only by renouncing society. All who had known Natásha before her marriage wondered at the change in her as at something extraordinary. Only the old countess with her maternal instinct had realized that all Natásha's outbursts had been due to her need of children and a husband—as she herself had once exclaimed at Otrádnoe not so much in fun as in earnest—and her mother was now surprised at the surprise expressed by those who had never understood Natásha, and she kept saying that she had always known that Natásha would make an exemplary wife and mother.

"Only she lets her love of her husband and children overflow all bounds," said the countess, "so that it even becomes absurd."

Natásha did not follow the golden rule advocated by clever folk, especially by the French, which says that a girl should not let herself go when she marries, should not neglect her accomplishments, should be even more careful of her appearance than when she was unmarried, and should fascinate her husband as much as she did before he became her husband. Natásha on the contrary had at once abandoned all her witchery, of which her singing had been an unusually powerful part. She gave it up just because it was so powerfully seductive. She took no pains with her manners or with delicacy of speech, or with her toilet, or to show herself to her husband in her most becoming attitudes, or to avoid inconveniencing him by being too exacting. She acted in contradiction to all those rules. She felt that the allurements instinct had formerly taught her to use would now be merely ridiculous in the eyes of her husband, to whom she had from the first moment given herself up entirely—that is, with her whole soul, leaving no corner of it hidden from him. She felt that her unity with her husband was not maintained by the poetic feelings that had attracted him to her, but by something else—indefinite but firm as the bond between her own body and soul.

To fluff out her curls, put on fashionable dresses, and sing romantic songs to fascinate her husband would have seemed as strange as to adorn herself to attract herself. To adorn herself for others might perhaps have been agreeable—she did not know—but she had no time at all for it. The chief reason for devoting no time either to singing, to dress, or to choosing her words was that she really had no time to spare for these things.

We know that man has the faculty of becoming completely absorbed in a subject however trivial it may be, and that there is no subject so trivial that it will not grow to infinite proportions if one's entire attention is devoted to it.

The subject which wholly engrossed Natásha's attention was her family: that is, her husband whom she had to keep so that he should belong entirely to her and to the home, and the children whom she had to bear, bring into the world, nurse, and bring up.

And the deeper she penetrated, not with her mind only but with her whole soul, her whole being, into the subject that absorbed her, the larger did that subject grow and the weaker and more inadequate did her powers appear, so that she concentrated them wholly on that one thing and yet was unable to accomplish all that she considered necessary.

There were then as now conversations and discussions about women's rights, the relations of husband and wife and their freedom and rights, though these themes were not yet termed *questions* as they are now; but these topics were not merely uninteresting to Natásha, she positively did not understand them.

These questions, then as now, existed only for those who see nothing in marriage but the pleasure married people get from one another, that is, only the beginnings of marriage and not its whole significance, which lies in the family.

Discussions and questions of that kind, which are like the question of how to get the greatest gratification from one's dinner, did not then and do not now exist for those for whom the purpose of a dinner is the nourishment it affords; and the purpose of marriage is the family.

If the purpose of dinner is to nourish the body, a man who eats two dinners at once may perhaps get more enjoyment but will not attain his purpose, for his stomach will not digest the two dinners.

If the purpose of marriage is the family, the person who wishes to have many wives or husbands may perhaps obtain much pleasure, but in that case will not have a family.

If the purpose of food is nourishment and the purpose of marriage is the family, the whole question resolves itself into not eating more than one can digest, and not having more wives or husbands than are needed for the family—that is, one wife or one husband. Natásha needed a husband. A husband was given her and he gave her a family. And she not only saw no need of any other or better husband, but as all the powers of her soul were intent on serving that husband and family, she could not imagine and saw no interest in imagining how it would be if things were different.

Natásha did not care for society in general, but prized the more the society of her relatives—Countess Mary, and her brother, her mother, and Sónya. She valued the company of those to whom she could come striding disheveled from the nursery in her dressing gown, and with joyful face show a yellow instead of a green stain on baby's napkin, and from whom she could hear reassuring words to the effect that baby was much better.

To such an extent had Natásha let herself go that the way she dressed and did her hair, her ill-chosen words, and her jealousy—she was jealous of Sónya, of the governess, and of every woman, pretty or plain—were habitual subjects of jest to those about her. The general opinion was that Pierre was under his wife's thumb, which was really true. From the very first days of their married life Natásha had announced her demands. Pierre was greatly surprised by his wife's view, to him a perfectly novel one, that every moment of his life belonged to her and to the family. His wife's demands astonished him, but they also flattered him, and he submitted to them.

Pierre's subjection consisted in the fact that he not only dared not flirt with, but dared not even speak smilingly to, any other woman; did not dare dine at the Club as a pastime, did not dare spend money on a whim, and did not dare absent himself for any length of time, except on business—in which his wife included his intellectual pursuits, which she did not in the least understand but to which she attributed great importance. To make up for this, at home Pierre had the right to regulate his life and that of the whole family exactly as he chose. At home Natásha placed herself in the position of a slave to her husband, and the whole household went on tiptoe when he was occupied—that is, was reading or writing in his study. Pierre had but to show a partiality for anything to get just what he liked done always. He had only to express a wish and Natásha would jump up and run to fulfill it.

The entire household was governed according to Pierre's supposed orders, that is, by his wishes which Natásha tried to guess. Their way of life and place of residence, their acquaintances and ties,

Natásha's occupations, the children's upbringing, were all selected not merely with regard to Pierre's expressed wishes, but to what Natásha from the thoughts he expressed in conversation supposed his wishes to be. And she deduced the essentials of his wishes quite correctly, and having once arrived at them clung to them tenaciously. When Pierre himself wanted to change his mind she would fight him with his own weapons.

Thus in a time of trouble ever memorable to him after the birth of their first child who was delicate, when they had to change the wet nurse three times and Natásha fell ill from despair, Pierre one day told her of Rousseau's view, with which he quite agreed, that to have a wet nurse is unnatural and harmful. When her next baby was born, despite the opposition of her mother, the doctors, and even of her husband himself—who were all vigorously opposed to her nursing her baby herself, a thing then unheard of and considered injurious—she insisted on having her own way, and after that nursed all her babies herself.

It very often happened that in a moment of irritation husband and wife would have a dispute, but long afterwards Pierre to his surprise and delight would find in his wife's ideas and actions the very thought against which she had argued, but divested of everything superfluous that in the excitement of the dispute he had added when expressing his opinion.

After seven years of marriage Pierre had the joyous and firm consciousness that he was not a bad man, and he felt this because he saw himself reflected in his wife. He felt the good and bad within himself inextricably mingled and overlapping. But only what was really good in him was reflected in his wife, all that was not quite good was rejected. And this was not the result of logical reasoning but was a direct and mysterious reflection.

CHAPTER XI

Two months previously when Pierre was already staying with the Rostóvs he had received a letter from Prince Theodore, asking him to come to Petersburg to confer on some important questions that were being discussed there by a society of which Pierre was one of the principal founders.

On reading that letter (she always read her husband's letters) Natásha herself suggested that he should go to Petersburg, though she would feel his absence very acutely. She attributed immense importance to all her husband's intellectual and abstract interests though she did not understand them, and she always dreaded being a hindrance to him in such matters. To Pierre's timid look of inquiry after reading the letter she replied by asking him to go, but to fix a definite date for his return. He was given four weeks' leave of absence.

Ever since that leave of absence had expired, more than a fortnight before, Natásha had been in a constant state of alarm, depression, and irritability.

Denísov, now a general on the retired list and much dissatisfied with the present state of affairs, had arrived during that fortnight. He looked at Natásha with sorrow and surprise as at a bad likeness of a person once dear. A dull, dejected look, random replies, and talk about the nursery was all he saw and heard from his former enchantress.

Natásha was sad and irritable all that time, especially when her mother, her brother, Sónya, or Countess Mary in their efforts to console her tried to excuse Pierre and suggested reasons for his delay in returning.

"It's all nonsense, all rubbish—those discussions which lead to nothing and all those idiotic societies!" Natásha declared of the very affairs in the immense importance of which she firmly believed. And she would go to the nursery to nurse Pétya, her only boy. No one else could tell her anything so comforting or so reasonable as this little three-month-old creature when he lay at her breast and she was conscious of the movement of his lips and the snuffling of his little nose. That creature said: "You are angry, you are jealous, you would like to pay him out, you are afraid—but here am I! And I am he..." and that was unanswerable. It was more than true.

During that fortnight of anxiety Natásha resorted to the baby for comfort so often, and fussed over him so much, that she overfed him and he fell ill. She was terrified by his illness, and yet that was just what she needed. While attending to him she bore the anxiety about her husband more easily.

She was nursing her boy when the sound of Pierre's sleigh was heard at the front door, and the old nurse—knowing how to please her mistress—entered the room inaudibly but hurriedly and with a beaming face.

"Has he come?" Natásha asked quickly in a whisper, afraid to move lest she should rouse the dozing baby.

"He's come, ma'am," whispered the nurse.

The blood rushed to Natásha's face and her feet involuntarily moved, but she could not jump up and run out. The baby again opened his eyes and looked at her. "You're here?" he seemed to be saying, and again lazily smacked his lips.

Cautiously withdrawing her breast, Natásha rocked him a little, handed him to the nurse, and went with rapid steps toward the door. But at the door she stopped as if her conscience reproached her for having in her joy left the child too soon, and she glanced round. The nurse with raised elbows was lifting the infant over the rail of his cot.

"Go, ma'am! Don't worry, go!" she whispered, smiling, with the kind of familiarity that grows up between a nurse and her mistress.

Natásha ran with light footsteps to the anteroom.

Denísov, who had come out of the study into the dancing room with his pipe, now for the first time recognized the old Natásha. A flood of brilliant, joyful light poured from her transfigured face.

"He's come!" she exclaimed as she ran past, and Denísov felt that he too was delighted that Pierre, whom he did not much care for, had returned.

On reaching the vestibule Natásha saw a tall figure in a fur coat unwinding his scarf. "It's he! It's really he! He has come!" she said to herself, and rushing at him embraced him, pressed his head to her breast, and then pushed him back and gazed at his ruddy, happy face, covered with hoarfrost. "Yes, it is he, happy and contented...."

Then all at once she remembered the tortures of suspense she had experienced for the last fortnight, and the joy that had lit up her face vanished; she frowned and overwhelmed Pierre with a torrent of reproaches and angry words.

"Yes, it's all very well for you. You are pleased, you've had a good time.... But what about me? You might at least have shown consideration for the children. I am nursing and my milk was spoiled.... Pétya was at death's door. But you were enjoying yourself. Yes, enjoying..."

Pierre knew he was not to blame, for he could not have come sooner; he knew this outburst was unseemly and would blow over in a minute or two; above all he knew that he himself was bright and happy. He wanted to smile but dared not even think of doing so. He made a piteous, frightened face and bent down.

"I could not, on my honor. But how is Pétya?"

"All right now. Come along! I wonder you're not ashamed! If only you could see what I was like without you, how I suffered!"

"You are well?"

"Come, come!" she said, not letting go of his arm. And they went to their rooms.

When Nicholas and his wife came to look for Pierre he was in the nursery holding his baby son, who was again awake, on his huge right palm and dandling him. A blissful bright smile was fixed on the baby's broad face with its toothless open mouth. The storm was long since over and there was bright, joyous sunshine on Natásha's face as she gazed tenderly at her husband and child.

"And have you talked everything well over with Prince Theodore?" she asked.

"Yes, capitally."

"You see, he holds it up." (She meant the baby's head.) "But how he did frighten me... You've seen the princess? Is it true she's in love with that..."

"Yes, just fancy..."

At that moment Nicholas and Countess Mary came in. Pierre with the baby on his hand stooped, kissed them, and replied to their inquiries. But in spite of much that was interesting and had to be discussed, the baby with the little cap on its unsteady head evidently absorbed all his attention.

"How sweet!" said Countess Mary, looking at and playing with the baby. "Now, Nicholas," she added, turning to her husband, "I can't understand how it is you don't see the charm of these delicious marvels."

"I don't and can't," replied Nicholas, looking coldly at the baby. "A lump of flesh. Come along, Pierre!"

"And yet he's such an affectionate father," said Countess Mary, vindicating her husband, "but only after they are a year old or so..."

"Now, Pierre nurses them splendidly," said Natásha. "He says his hand is just made for a baby's seat. Just look!"

"Only not for this..." Pierre suddenly exclaimed with a laugh, and shifting the baby he gave him to the nurse.

CHAPTER XII

As in every large household, there were at Bald Hills several perfectly distinct worlds which merged into one harmonious whole, though each retained its own peculiarities and made concessions to the others. Every event, joyful or sad, that took place in that house was important to all these worlds, but each had its own special reasons to rejoice or grieve over that occurrence independently of the others.

For instance, Pierre's return was a joyful and important event and they all felt it to be so.

The servants—the most reliable judges of their masters because they judge not by their conversation or expressions of feeling but by their acts and way of life—were glad of Pierre's return because they knew that when he was there Count Nicholas would cease going every day to attend to the estate, and would be in better spirits and temper, and also because they would all receive handsome presents for the holidays.

The children and their governesses were glad of Pierre's return because no one else drew them into the social life of the household as he did. He alone could play on the clavichord that *écossaise* (his only piece) to which, as he said, all possible dances could be danced, and they felt sure he had brought presents for them all.

Young Nicholas, now a slim lad of fifteen, delicate and intelligent, with curly light-brown hair and beautiful eyes, was delighted because Uncle Pierre as he called him was the object of his rapturous and passionate affection. No one had instilled into him this love for Pierre whom he saw only occasionally. Countess Mary who had brought him up had done her utmost to make him love her husband as she loved him, and little Nicholas did love his uncle, but loved him with just a shade of contempt. Pierre, however, he adored. He did not want to be an hussar or a Knight of St. George like his uncle Nicholas; he wanted to be learned, wise, and kind like Pierre. In Pierre's presence his face always shone with pleasure and he flushed and was breathless when Pierre spoke to him. He did not miss a single word he uttered, and would afterwards, with Dessalles or by himself, recall and reconsider the meaning of everything Pierre had said. Pierre's past life and his unhappiness prior to 1812 (of which young Nicholas had formed a vague poetic picture from some words he had overheard), his adventures in Moscow, his captivity, PlatónKaratáev (of whom he had heard from Pierre), his love for Natásha (of whom the lad was also particularly fond), and especially Pierre's friendship with the father whom Nicholas could not remember—all this made Pierre in his eyes a hero and a saint.

From broken remarks about Natásha and his father, from the emotion with which Pierre spoke of that dead father, and from the careful, reverent tenderness with which Natásha spoke of him, the boy, who was only just beginning to guess what love is, derived the notion that his father had loved Natásha and when dying had left her to his friend. But the father whom the boy did not remember appeared to him a divinity who could not be pictured, and of whom he never thought without a swelling heart and tears of sadness and rapture. So the boy also was happy that Pierre had arrived.

The guests welcomed Pierre because he always helped to enliven and unite any company he was in.

The grown-up members of the family, not to mention his wife, were pleased to have back a friend whose presence made life run more smoothly and peacefully.

The old ladies were pleased with the presents he brought them, and especially that Natásha would now be herself again.

Pierre felt the different outlooks of these various worlds and made haste to satisfy all their expectations.

Though the most absent-minded and forgetful of men, Pierre, with the aid of a list his wife drew up, had now bought everything, not forgetting his mother—and brother-in-law's commissions, nor the dress material for a present to Belóva, nor toys for his wife's nephews. In the early days of his marriage it had seemed strange to him that his wife should expect him not to forget to procure all the things he undertook to buy, and he had been taken aback by her serious annoyance when on his first trip he forgot everything. But in time he grew used to this demand. Knowing that Natásha asked nothing for herself, and gave him commissions for others only when he himself had offered to undertake them, he now found an unexpected and childlike pleasure in this purchase of presents for everyone in the house, and never forgot anything. If he now incurred Natásha's censure it was only for buying too many and too expensive things. To her other defects (as most people thought them, but which to Pierre were qualities) of untidiness and neglect of herself, she now added stinginess.

From the time that Pierre began life as a family man on a footing entailing heavy expenditure, he had noticed to his surprise that he spent only half as much as before, and that his affairs—which had been in disorder of late, chiefly because of his first wife's debts—had begun to improve.

Life was cheaper because it was circumscribed: that most expensive luxury, the kind of life that can be changed at any moment, was no longer his nor did he wish for it. He felt that his way of life had now been settled once for all till death and that to change it was not in his power, and so that way of life proved economical.

With a merry, smiling face Pierre was sorting his purchases.

"What do you think of this?" said he, unrolling a piece of stuff like a shopman.

Natásha, who was sitting opposite to him with her eldest daughter on her lap, turned her sparkling eyes swiftly from her husband to the things he showed her.

"That's for Belóva? Excellent!" She felt the quality of the material. "It was a ruble an arshin, I suppose?"

Pierre told her the price.

"Too dear!" Natásha remarked. "How pleased the children will be and Mamma too! Only you need not have bought me this," she added, unable to suppress a smile as she gazed admiringly at a gold comb set with pearls, of a kind then just coming into fashion.

"Adèle tempted me: she kept on telling me to buy it," returned Pierre.

"When am I to wear it?" and Natásha stuck it in her coil of hair. "When I take little Másha into society? Perhaps they will be fashionable again by then. Well, let's go now."

And collecting the presents they went first to the nursery and then to the old countess' rooms.

The countess was sitting with her companion Belóva, playing grand-patience as usual, when Pierre and Natásha came into the drawing room with parcels under their arms.

The countess was now over sixty, was quite gray, and wore a cap with a frill that surrounded her face. Her face had shriveled, her upper lip had sunk in, and her eyes were dim.

After the deaths of her son and husband in such rapid succession, she felt herself a being accidentally forgotten in this world and left without aim or object for her existence. She ate, drank, slept, or kept awake, but did not *live*. Life gave her no new impressions. She wanted nothing from life but tranquillity, and that tranquillity only death could give her. But until death came she had to go on living, that is, to use her vital forces. A peculiarity one sees in very young children and very old people was particularly evident in her. Her life had no external aims—only a need to exercise her various functions and inclinations was apparent. She had to eat, sleep, think, speak, weep, work, give vent to her anger, and so on, merely because she had a stomach, a brain, muscles, nerves, and a liver. She did these things not under any external impulse as people in the full vigor of life do, when behind the purpose for which they strive that of exercising their functions remains unnoticed. She talked only because she physically needed to exercise her tongue and lungs. She cried as a child does, because her nose had to be cleared, and so on. What for people in their full vigor is an aim was for her evidently merely a pretext.

Thus in the morning—especially if she had eaten anything rich the day before—she felt a need of being angry and would choose as the handiest pretext Belóva's deafness.

She would begin to say something to her in a low tone from the other end of the room.

"It seems a little warmer today, my dear," she would murmur.

And when Belóva replied: "Oh yes, they've come," she would mutter angrily: "O Lord! How stupid and deaf she is!"

Another pretext would be her snuff, which would seem too dry or too damp or not rubbed fine enough. After these fits of irritability her face would grow yellow, and her maids knew by infallible symptoms when Belóva would again be deaf, the snuff damp, and the countess' face yellow. Just as she needed to work off her spleen so she had sometimes to exercise her still-existing faculty of thinking—and the pretext for that was a game of patience. When she needed to cry, the deceased count would be the pretext. When she wanted to be agitated, Nicholas and his health would be the pretext, and when she felt a need to speak spitefully, the pretext would be Countess Mary. When her vocal organs needed exercise, which was usually toward seven o'clock when she had had an after-dinner rest in a darkened room, the pretext would be the retelling of the same stories over and over again to the same audience.

The old lady's condition was understood by the whole household though no one ever spoke of it, and they all made every possible effort to satisfy her needs. Only by a rare glance exchanged with a sad smile between Nicholas, Pierre, Natásha, and Countess Mary was the common understanding of her condition expressed.

But those glances expressed something more: they said that she had played her part in life, that what they now saw was not her whole self, that we must all become like her, and that they were glad to yield to her, to restrain themselves for this once precious being formerly as full of life as themselves, but now so much to be pitied. *"Memento mori,"* said these glances.

Only the really heartless, the stupid ones of that household, and the little children failed to understand this and avoided her.

CHAPTER XIII

W hen Pierre and his wife entered the drawing room the countess was in one of her customary states in which she needed the mental exertion of playing patience, and so—though by force of habit she greeted him with the words she always used when Pierre or her son returned after an absence: "High time, my dear, high time! We were all weary of waiting for you. Well, thank God!" and received her presents with another customary remark: "It's not the gift that's precious, my dear, but that you give it to me, an old woman..."—yet it was evident that she was not pleased by Pierre's arrival at that moment when it diverted her attention from the unfinished game.

She finished her game of patience and only then examined the presents. They consisted of a box for cards, of splendid workmanship, a bright-blue Sèvres tea cup with shepherdesses depicted on it and with a lid, and a gold snuffbox with the count's portrait on the lid which Pierre had had done by a miniaturist in Petersburg. The countess had long wished for such a box, but as she did not want to cry just then she glanced indifferently at the portrait and gave her attention chiefly to the box for cards.

"Thank you, my dear, you have cheered me up," said she as she always did. "But best of all you have brought yourself back—for I never saw anything like it, you ought to give your wife a scolding! What are we to do with her? She is like a mad woman when you are away. Doesn't see anything, doesn't remember anything," she went on, repeating her usual phrases. "Look, Anna Timoféevna," she added to her companion, "see what a box for cards my son has brought us!"

Belóva admired the presents and was delighted with her dress material.

Though Pierre, Natásha, Nicholas, Countess Mary, and Denísov had much to talk about that they could not discuss before the old countess—not that anything was hidden from her, but because she had dropped so far behindhand in many things that had they begun to converse in her presence they would have had to answer inopportune questions and to repeat what they had already told her many times: that so-and-so was dead and so-and-so was married, which she would again be unable to remember—yet they sat at tea round the samovar in the drawing room from habit, and Pierre answered the countess' questions as to whether Prince Vasíli had aged and whether Countess Mary Alexéevna had sent greetings and still thought of them, and other matters that interested no one and to which she herself was indifferent.

Conversation of this kind, interesting to no one yet unavoidable, continued all through teatime. All the grown-up members of the family were assembled near the round tea table at which Sónya presided beside the samovar. The children with their tutors and governesses had had tea and their voices were audible from the next room. At tea all sat in their accustomed places: Nicholas beside the stove at a small table where his tea was handed to him; Mílka, the old gray borzoi bitch (daughter of the first Mílka), with a quite gray face and large black eyes that seemed more prominent than ever, lay on the armchair beside him; Denísov, whose curly hair, mustache, and whiskers had turned half gray, sat beside countess Mary with his general's tunic unbuttoned; Pierre sat between his wife and the old countess. He spoke of what he knew might interest the old lady and that she could understand. He told her of external social events and of the people who had formed the circle of her contemporaries and had once been a real, living, and distinct group, but who were now for the most part scattered about the world and like herself were garnering the last ears of the harvests they had sown in earlier years. But to the old countess those contemporaries of hers seemed to be the only serious and real society. Natásha saw by Pierre's animation that his visit had been interesting and that he had much to tell them but dare not say it before the old countess. Denísov, not being a member of the family, did not understand Pierre's caution and being, as a malcontent, much interested in what was occurring in Petersburg, kept urging Pierre to tell them about what had happened in the Semënovsk regiment, then about Arakchéev, and then about the Bible Society. Once or twice Pierre was carried away and began to speak of these things, but Nicholas and Natásha always brought him back to the health of Prince Iván and Countess Mary Alexéevna.

"Well, and all this idiocy—Gossner and Tatáwinova?" Denísov asked. "Is that weally still going on?"

"Going on?" Pierre exclaimed. "Why more than ever! The Bible Society is the whole government now!"

"What is that, *moncherami?*" asked the countess, who had finished her tea and evidently needed a pretext for being angry after her meal. "What are you saying about the government? I don't understand."

"Well, you know, *Maman*," Nicholas interposed, knowing how to translate things into his mother's language, "Prince Alexander Golítsyn has founded a society and in consequence has great influence, they say."

"Arakchéev and Golítsyn," incautiously remarked Pierre, "are now the whole government! And what a government! They see treason everywhere and are afraid of everything."

"Well, and how is Prince Alexander to blame? He is a most estimable man. I used to meet him at Mary Antónovna's," said the countess in an offended tone; and still more offended that they all remained silent, she went on: "Nowadays everyone finds fault. A Gospel Society! Well, and what harm is there in that?" and she rose (everybody else got up too) and with a severe expression sailed back to her table in the sitting room.

The melancholy silence that followed was broken by the sounds of the children's voices and laughter from the next room. Evidently some jolly excitement was going on there.

"Finished, finished!" little Natásha's gleeful yell rose above them all.

Pierre exchanged glances with Countess Mary and Nicholas (Natásha he never lost sight of) and smiled happily.

"That's delightful music!" said he.

"It means that Anna Makárovna has finished her stocking," said Countess Mary.

"Oh, I'll go and see," said Pierre, jumping up. "You know," he added, stopping at the door, "why I'm especially fond of that music? It is always the first thing that tells me all is well. When I was driving here today, the nearer I got to the house the more anxious I grew. As I entered the anteroom I heard Andrúsha's peals of laughter and that meant that all was well."

"I know! I know that feeling," said Nicholas. "But I mustn't go there—those stockings are to be a surprise for me."

Pierre went to the children, and the shouting and laughter grew still louder.

"Come, Anna Makárovna," Pierre's voice was heard saying, "come here into the middle of the room and at the word of command, 'One, two,' and when I say 'three'... You stand here, and you in my arms—well now! One, two!..." said Pierre, and a silence followed: "three!" and a rapturously breathless cry of children's voices filled the room. "Two, two!" they shouted.

This meant two stockings, which by a secret process known only to herself Anna Makárovna used to knit at the same time on the same needles, and which, when they were ready, she always triumphantly drew, one out of the other, in the children's presence.

CHAPTER XIV

Soon after this the children came in to say good night. They kissed everyone, the tutors and governesses made their bows, and they went out. Only young Nicholas and his tutor remained. Dessalles whispered to the boy to come downstairs.

"No, Monsieur Dessalles, I will ask my aunt to let me stay," replied Nicholas Bolkónski also in a whisper.

"*Ma tante*, please let me stay," said he, going up to his aunt.

His face expressed entreaty, agitation, and ecstasy. Countess Mary glanced at him and turned to Pierre.

"When you are here he can't tear himself away," she said.

"I will bring him to you directly, Monsieur Dessalles. Good night!" said Pierre, giving his hand to the Swiss tutor, and he turned to young Nicholas with a smile. "You and I haven't seen anything of one another yet.... How like he is growing, Mary!" he added, addressing Countess Mary.

"Like my father?" asked the boy, flushing crimson and looking up at Pierre with bright, ecstatic eyes.

Pierre nodded, and went on with what he had been saying when the children had interrupted. Countess Mary sat down doing woolwork; Natásha did not take her eyes off her husband. Nicholas and Denísov rose, asked for their pipes, smoked, went to fetch more tea from Sónya—who sat weary but resolute at the samovar—and questioned Pierre. The curly-headed, delicate boy sat with shining eyes unnoticed in a corner, starting every now and then and muttering something to himself, and evidently experiencing a new and powerful emotion as he turned his curly head, with his thin neck exposed by his turn-down collar, toward the place where Pierre sat.

The conversation turned on the contemporary gossip about those in power, in which most people see the chief interest of home politics. Denísov, dissatisfied with the government on account of his own disappointments in the service, heard with pleasure of the things done in Petersburg which seemed to him stupid, and made forcible and sharp comments on what Pierre told them.

"One used to have to be a German—now one must dance with Tatáwinova and Madame Kwüdener, and weadEcka'tshausen and the bwethwen. Oh, they should let that fine fellow Bonaparte loose—he'd knock all this nonsense out of them! Fancy giving the command of the Semënovwegiment to a fellow like that Schwa'tz!" he cried.

Nicholas, though free from Denísov's readiness to find fault with everything, also thought that discussion of the government was a very serious and weighty matter, and the fact that *A* had been appointed Minister of This and *B* Governor General of That, and that the Emperor had said so-and-so and this minister so-and-so, seemed to him very important. And so he thought it necessary to take an interest in these things and to question Pierre. The questions put by these two kept the conversation from changing its ordinary character of gossip about the higher government circles.

But Natásha, knowing all her husband's ways and ideas, saw that he had long been wishing but had been unable to divert the conversation to another channel and express his own deeply felt idea for the sake of which he had gone to Petersburg to consult with his new friend Prince Theodore, and she helped him by asking how his affairs with Prince Theodore had gone.

"What was it about?" asked Nicholas.

"Always the same thing," said Pierre, looking round at his listeners. "Everybody sees that things are going so badly that they cannot be allowed to go on so and that it is the duty of all decent men to counteract it as far as they can."

"What can decent men do?" Nicholas inquired, frowning slightly. "What can be done?"

"Why, this..."

"Come into my study," said Nicholas.

Natásha, who had long expected to be fetched to nurse her baby, now heard the nurse calling her and went to the nursery. Countess Mary followed her. The men went into the study and little Nicholas Bolkónski followed them unnoticed by his uncle and sat down at the writing table in a shady corner by the window.

"Well, what would you do?" asked Denísov.

"Always some fantastic schemes," said Nicholas.

"Why this," began Pierre, not sitting down but pacing the room, sometimes stopping short, gesticulating, and lisping: "the position in Petersburg is this: the Emperor does not look into anything. He has abandoned himself altogether to this mysticism" (Pierre could not tolerate mysticism in anyone now). "He seeks only for peace, and only these people *sans foiniloi* * can give it him—people who recklessly hack at and strangle everything—Magnítski, Arakchéev, and *tutti quanti*.... You will agree that if you did not look after your estates yourself but only wanted a quiet life, the harsher your steward was the more readily your object might be attained," he said to Nicholas.

* Without faith or law.

"Well, what does that lead up to?" said Nicholas.

"Well, everything is going to ruin! Robbery in the law courts, in the army nothing but flogging, drilling, and Military Settlements; the people are tortured, enlightenment is suppressed. All that is young and honest is crushed! Everyone sees that this cannot go on. Everything is strained to such a degree that it will certainly break," said Pierre (as those who examine the actions of any government have always said since governments began). "I told them just one thing in Petersburg."

"Told whom?"

"Well, you know whom," said Pierre, with a meaning glance from under his brows. "Prince Theodore and all those. To encourage culture and philanthropy is all very well of course. The aim is excellent but in the present circumstances something else is needed."

At that moment Nicholas noticed the presence of his nephew. His face darkened and he went up to the boy.

"Why are you here?"

"Why? Let him be," said Pierre, taking Nicholas by the arm and continuing. "That is not enough, I told them. Something else is needed.

When you stand expecting the overstrained string to snap at any moment, when everyone is expecting the inevitable catastrophe, as many as possible must join hands as closely as they can to withstand the general calamity. Everything that is young and strong is being enticed away and depraved. One is lured by women, another by honors, a third by ambition or money, and they go over to that camp. No independent men, such as you or I, are left. What I say is widen the scope of our society, let the *mot d'ordre* be not virtue alone but independence and action as well!"

Nicholas, who had left his nephew, irritably pushed up an armchair, sat down in it, and listened to Pierre, coughing discontentedly and frowning more and more.

"But action with what aim?" he cried. "And what position will you adopt toward the government?"

"Why, the position of assistants. The society need not be secret if the government allows it. Not merely is it not hostile to government, but it is a society of true conservatives—a society of gentlemen in the full meaning of that word. It is only to prevent some Pugachëv or other from killing my children and yours, and Arakchéev from sending me off to some Military Settlement. We join hands only for the public welfare and the general safety."

"Yes, but it's a secret society and therefore a hostile and harmful one which can only cause harm."

"Why? Did the Tugendbund which saved Europe" (they did not then venture to suggest that Russia had saved Europe) "do any harm? The Tugendbund is an alliance of virtue: it is love, mutual help... it is what Christ preached on the Cross."

Natásha, who had come in during the conversation, looked joyfully at her husband. It was not what he was saying that pleased her—that did not even interest her, for it seemed to her that was all extremely simple and that she had known it a long time (it seemed so to her because she knew that it sprang from Pierre's whole soul), but it was his animated and enthusiastic appearance that made her glad.

The boy with the thin neck stretching out from the turn-down collar—whom everyone had forgotten—gazed at Pierre with even greater and more rapturous joy. Every word of Pierre's burned into his heart, and with a nervous movement of his fingers he unconsciously broke the sealing wax and quill pens his hands came upon on his uncle's table.

"It is not at all what you suppose; but that is what the German Tugendbund was, and what I am proposing."

"No, my fwiend! The Tugendbund is all vewy well for the sausage eaters, but I don't understand it and can't even pwonounce it," interposed Denísov in a loud and resolute voice. "I agwee that evewything here is wotten and howwible, but the *Tugendbund* I don't understand. If we're not satisfied, let us have a *bunt* of our own. That's all wight. *Je suisvot'e homme!"* *

* "I'm your man."

Pierre smiled, Natásha began to laugh, but Nicholas knitted his brows still more and began proving to Pierre that there was no prospect of any great change and that all the danger he spoke of existed only in his imagination. Pierre maintained the contrary, and as his mental faculties were greater and more resourceful, Nicholas felt himself cornered. This made him still angrier, for he was fully convinced, not by reasoning but by something within him stronger than reason, of the justice of his opinion.

"I will tell you this," he said, rising and trying with nervously twitching fingers to prop up his pipe in a corner, but finally abandoning the attempt. "I can't prove it to you. You say that everything here is rotten and that an overthrow is coming: I don't see it. But you also say that our oath of allegiance is a conditional matter, and to that I reply: 'You are my best friend, as you know, but if you formed a secret society and began working against the government—be it what it may—I know it is my duty to obey the government. And if Arakchéev ordered me to lead a squadron against you and cut you down, I should not hesitate an instant, but should do it.' And you may argue about that as you like!"

An awkward silence followed these words. Natásha was the first to speak, defending her husband and attacking her brother. Her defense was weak and inapt but she attained her object. The conversation was resumed, and no longer in the unpleasantly hostile tone of Nicholas' last remark.

When they all got up to go in to supper, little Nicholas Bolkónski went up to Pierre, pale and with shining, radiant eyes.

"Uncle Pierre, you... no... If Papa were alive... would he agree with you?" he asked.

And Pierre suddenly realized what a special, independent, complex, and powerful process of thought and feeling must have been going on in this boy during that conversation, and remembering all he had said he regretted that the lad should have heard him. He had, however, to give him an answer.

"Yes, I think so," he said reluctantly, and left the study.

The lad looked down and seemed now for the first time to notice what he had done to the things on the table. He flushed and went up to Nicholas.

"Uncle, forgive me, I did that... unintentionally," he said, pointing to the broken sealing wax and pens.

Nicholas started angrily.

"All right, all right," he said, throwing the bits under the table.

And evidently suppressing his vexation with difficulty, he turned away from the boy.

"You ought not to have been here at all," he said.

CHAPTER XV

The conversation at supper was not about politics or societies, but turned on the subject Nicholas liked best—recollections of 1812. Denísov started these and Pierre was particularly agreeable and amusing about them. The family separated on the most friendly terms.

After supper Nicholas, having undressed in his study and given instructions to the steward who had been waiting for him, went to the bedroom in his dressing gown, where he found his wife still at her table, writing.

"What are you writing, Mary?" Nicholas asked.

Countess Mary blushed. She was afraid that what she was writing would not be understood or approved by her husband.

She had wanted to conceal what she was writing from him, but at the same time was glad he had surprised her at it and that she would now have to tell him.

"A diary, Nicholas," she replied, handing him a blue exercise book filled with her firm, bold writing.

"A diary?" Nicholas repeated with a shade of irony, and he took up the book.

It was in French.

December 4. Today when Andrúsha (her eldest boy) woke up he did not wish to dress and Mademoiselle Louise sent for me. He was naughty and obstinate. I tried threats, but he only grew angrier. Then I took the matter in hand: I left him alone and began with nurse's help to get the other children up, telling him that I did not love him. For a long time he was silent, as if astonished, then he jumped out of bed, ran to me in his shirt, and sobbed so that I could not calm him for a long time. It was plain that what troubled him most was that he had grieved me. Afterwards in the evening when I gave him his ticket, he again began crying piteously and kissing me. One can do anything with him by tenderness.

"What is a 'ticket'?" Nicholas inquired.

"I have begun giving the elder ones marks every evening, showing how they have behaved."

Nicholas looked into the radiant eyes that were gazing at him, and continued to turn over the pages and read. In the diary was set down everything in the children's lives that seemed noteworthy to their mother as showing their characters or suggesting general reflections on educational methods. They were for the most part quite insignificant trifles, but did not seem so to the mother or to the father either, now that he read this diary about his children for the first time.

Under the date "5" was entered:

Mítya was naughty at table. Papa said he was to have no pudding. He had none, but looked so unhappily and greedily at the others while they were eating! I think that punishment by depriving children of sweets only develops their greediness. Must tell Nicholas this.

Nicholas put down the book and looked at his wife. The radiant eyes gazed at him questioningly: would he approve or disapprove of her diary? There could be no doubt not only of his approval but also of his admiration for his wife.

Perhaps it need not be done so pedantically, thought Nicholas, or even done at all, but this untiring, continual spiritual effort of which the sole aim was the children's moral welfare delighted him. Had

Nicholas been able to analyze his feelings he would have found that his steady, tender, and proud love of his wife rested on his feeling of wonder at her spirituality and at the lofty moral world, almost beyond his reach, in which she had her being.

He was proud of her intelligence and goodness, recognized his own insignificance beside her in the spiritual world, and rejoiced all the more that she with such a soul not only belonged to him but was part of himself.

"I quite, quite approve, my dearest!" said he with a significant look, and after a short pause he added: "And I behaved badly today. You weren't in the study. We began disputing—Pierre and I—and I lost my temper. But he is impossible: such a child! I don't know what would become of him if Natásha didn't keep him in hand.... Have you any idea why he went to Petersburg? They have formed..."

"Yes, I know," said Countess Mary. "Natásha told me."

"Well, then, you know," Nicholas went on, growing hot at the mere recollection of their discussion, "he wanted to convince me that it is every honest man's duty to go against the government, and that the oath of allegiance and duty... I am sorry you weren't there. They all fell on me—Denísov and Natásha... Natásha is absurd. How she rules over him! And yet there need only be a discussion and she has no words of her own but only repeats his sayings..." added Nicholas, yielding to that irresistible inclination which tempts us to judge those nearest and dearest to us. He forgot that what he was saying about Natásha could have been applied word for word to himself in relation to his wife.

"Yes, I have noticed that," said Countess Mary.

"When I told him that duty and the oath were above everything, he started proving goodness knows what! A pity you were not there—what would you have said?"

"As I see it you were quite right, and I told Natásha so. Pierre says everybody is suffering, tortured, and being corrupted, and that it is our duty to help our neighbor. Of course he is right there," said Countess Mary, "but he forgets that we have other duties nearer to us, duties indicated to us by God Himself, and that though we might expose ourselves to risks we must not risk our children."

"Yes, that's it! That's just what I said to him," put in Nicholas, who fancied he really had said it. "But they insisted on their own view: love of one's neighbor and Christianity—and all this in the presence of young Nicholas, who had gone into my study and broke all my things."

"Ah, Nicholas, do you know I am often troubled about little Nicholas," said Countess Mary. "He is such an exceptional boy. I am afraid I neglect him in favor of my own: we all have children and relations while he has no one. He is constantly alone with his thoughts."

"Well, I don't think you need reproach yourself on his account. All that the fondest mother could do for her son you have done and are doing for him, and of course I am glad of it. He is a fine lad, a fine lad! This evening he listened to Pierre in a sort of trance, and fancy— as we were going in to supper I looked and he had broken everything on my table to bits, and he told me of it himself at once! I never knew him to tell an untruth. A fine lad, a fine lad!" repeated Nicholas, who at heart was not fond of Nicholas Bolkónski but was always anxious to recognize that he was a fine lad.

"Still, I am not the same as his own mother," said Countess Mary. "I feel I am not the same and it troubles me. A wonderful boy, but I am dreadfully afraid for him. It would be good for him to have companions."

"Well it won't be for long. Next summer I'll take him to Petersburg," said Nicholas. "Yes, Pierre always was a dreamer and always will be," he continued, returning to the talk in the study which had evidently disturbed him. "Well, what business is it of mine what goes on there—whether Arakchéev is bad, and all that? What business was it of mine when I married and was so deep in debt that I was threatened with prison, and had a mother who could not see or understand it? And then there are you and the children and our affairs. Is it for my own pleasure that I am at the farm or in the office from morning to night? No, but I know I must work to comfort my mother, to repay you, and not to leave the children such beggars as I was."

Countess Mary wanted to tell him that man does not live by bread alone and that he attached too much importance to these matters. But she knew she must not say this and that it would be useless to do so. She only took his hand and kissed it. He took this as a sign of approval and a confirmation of his thoughts, and after a few minutes' reflection continued to think aloud.

"You know, Mary, today Elias Mitrofánych" (this was his overseer) "came back from the Tambóv estate and told me they are already offering eighty thousand rubles for the forest."

And with an eager face Nicholas began to speak of the possibility of repurchasing Otrádnoe before long, and added: "Another ten years of life and I shall leave the children... in an excellent position."

Countess Mary listened to her husband and understood all that he told her. She knew that when he thought aloud in this way he would sometimes ask her what he had been saying, and be vexed if he noticed that she had been thinking about something else. But she had to force herself to attend, for what he was saying did not interest her at all. She looked at him and did not think, but felt, about something different. She felt a submissive tender love for this man who would never understand all that she understood, and this seemed to make her love for him still stronger and added a touch of passionate tenderness. Besides this feeling which absorbed her altogether and hindered her from following the details of her husband's plans, thoughts that had no connection with what he was saying flitted through her mind. She thought of her nephew. Her husband's account of the boy's agitation while Pierre was speaking struck her forcibly, and various traits of his gentle, sensitive character recurred to her mind; and while thinking of her nephew she thought also of her own children. She did not compare them with him, but compared her feeling for them with her feeling for him, and felt with regret that there was something lacking in her feeling for young Nicholas.

Sometimes it seemed to her that this difference arose from the difference in their ages, but she felt herself to blame toward him and promised in her heart to do better and to accomplish the impossible—in this life to love her husband, her children, little Nicholas, and all her neighbors, as Christ loved mankind. Countess Mary's soul always strove toward the infinite, the eternal, and the absolute, and could therefore never be at peace. A stern expression of the lofty, secret suffering of a soul burdened by the body appeared on her face. Nicholas gazed at her. "O God! What will become of us if she dies, as I always fear when her face is like that?" thought he, and placing himself before the icon he began to say his evening prayers.

CHAPTER XVI

Natásha and Pierre, left alone, also began to talk as only a husband and wife can talk, that is, with extraordinary clearness and rapidity, understanding and expressing each other's thoughts in ways contrary to all rules of logic, without premises, deductions, or conclusions, and in a quite peculiar way. Natásha was so used to this kind of talk with her husband that for her it was the surest sign of something being wrong between them if Pierre followed a line of logical reasoning. When he began proving anything, or talking argumentatively and calmly and she, led on by his example, began to do the same, she knew that they were on the verge of a quarrel.

From the moment they were alone and Natásha came up to him with wide-open happy eyes, and quickly seizing his head pressed it to her bosom, saying: "Now you are all mine, mine! You won't escape!"— from that moment this conversation began, contrary to all the laws of logic and contrary to them because quite different subjects were talked about at one and the same time. This simultaneous discussion of many topics did not prevent a clear understanding but on the contrary was the surest sign that they fully understood one another.

Just as in a dream when all is uncertain, unreasoning, and contradictory, except the feeling that guides the dream, so in this intercourse contrary to all laws of reason, the words themselves were not consecutive and clear but only the feeling that prompted them.

Natásha spoke to Pierre about her brother's life and doings, of how she had suffered and lacked life during his own absence, and of how she was fonder than ever of Mary, and how Mary was in every way better than herself. In saying this Natásha was sincere in acknowledging Mary's superiority, but at the same time by saying it she made a demand on Pierre that he should, all the same, prefer her to Mary and to all other women, and that now, especially after having seen many women in Petersburg, he should tell her so afresh.

Pierre, answering Natásha's words, told her how intolerable it had been for him to meet ladies at dinners and balls in Petersburg.

"I have quite lost the knack of talking to ladies," he said. "It was simply dull. Besides, I was very busy."

Natásha looked intently at him and went on:

"Mary is so splendid," she said. "How she understands children! It is as if she saw straight into their souls. Yesterday, for instance, Mítya was naughty..."

"How like his father he is," Pierre interjected.

Natásha knew why he mentioned Mítya's likeness to Nicholas: the recollection of his dispute with his brother-in-law was unpleasant and he wanted to know what Natásha thought of it.

"Nicholas has the weakness of never agreeing with anything not generally accepted. But I understand that you value what opens up a fresh line," said she, repeating words Pierre had once uttered.

"No, the chief point is that to Nicholas ideas and discussions are an amusement—almost a pastime," said Pierre. "For instance, he is collecting a library and has made it a rule not to buy a new book till he has read what he had already bought—Sismondi and Rousseau and Montesquieu," he added with a smile. "You know how much I..." he began to soften down what he had said; but Natásha interrupted him to show that this was unnecessary.

"So you say ideas are an amusement to him...."

"Yes, and for me nothing else is serious. All the time in Petersburg I saw everyone as in a dream. When I am taken up by a thought, all else is mere amusement."

"Ah, I'm so sorry I wasn't there when you met the children," said Natásha. "Which was most delighted? Lisa, I'm sure."

"Yes," Pierre replied, and went on with what was in his mind. "Nicholas says we ought not to think. But I can't help it. Besides, when I was in Petersburg I felt (I can say this to you) that the whole affair would go to pieces without me—everyone was pulling his own way. But I succeeded in uniting them all; and then my idea is so clear and simple. You see, I don't say that we ought to oppose this and that. We may be mistaken. What I say is: 'Join hands, you who love the right, and let there be but one banner—that of active virtue.' Prince Sergéy is a fine fellow and clever."

Natásha would have had no doubt as to the greatness of Pierre's idea, but one thing disconcerted her. "Can a man so important and necessary to society be also my husband? How did this happen?" She wished to express this doubt to him. "Now who could decide whether he is really cleverer than all the others?" she asked herself, and passed in review all those whom Pierre most respected. Judging by what he had said there was no one he had respected so highly as PlatónKaratáev.

"Do you know what I am thinking about?" she asked. "About PlatónKaratáev. Would he have approved of you now, do you think?"

Pierre was not at all surprised at this question. He understood his wife's line of thought.

"PlatónKaratáev?" he repeated, and pondered, evidently sincerely trying to imagine Karatáev's opinion on the subject. "He would not have understood... yet perhaps he would."

"I love you awfully!" Natásha suddenly said. "Awfully, awfully!"

"No, he would not have approved," said Pierre, after reflection. "What he would have approved of is our family life. He was always so anxious to find seemliness, happiness, and peace in everything, and I should have been proud to let him see us. There now—you talk of my absence, but you wouldn't believe what a special feeling I have for you after a separation...."

"Yes, I should think..." Natásha began.

"No, it's not that. I never leave off loving you. And one couldn't love more, but this is something special.... Yes, of course—" he did not finish because their eyes meeting said the rest.

"What nonsense it is," Natásha suddenly exclaimed, "about honeymoons, and that the greatest happiness is at first! On the contrary, now is the best of all. If only you did not go away! Do you remember how we quarreled? And it was always my fault. Always mine. And what we quarreled about—I don't even remember!"

"Always about the same thing," said Pierre with a smile. "Jealo..."

"Don't say it! I can't bear it!" Natásha cried, and her eyes glittered coldly and vindictively. "Did you see her?" she added, after a pause.

"No, and if I had I shouldn't have recognized her."

They were silent for a while.

"Oh, do you know? While you were talking in the study I was looking at you," Natásha began, evidently anxious to disperse the cloud that had come over them. "You are as like him as two peas—like the boy." (She meant her little son.) "Oh, it's time to go to him.... The milk's come.... But I'm sorry to leave you."

They were silent for a few seconds. Then suddenly turning to one another at the same time they both began to speak. Pierre began with self-satisfaction and enthusiasm, Natásha with a quiet, happy smile. Having interrupted one another they both stopped to let the other continue.

"No. What did you say? Go on, go on."

"No, you go on, I was talking nonsense," said Natásha.

Pierre finished what he had begun. It was the sequel to his complacent reflections on his success in Petersburg. At that moment it seemed to him that he was chosen to give a new direction to the whole of Russian society and to the whole world.

"I only wished to say that ideas that have great results are always simple ones. My whole idea is that if vicious people are united and constitute a power, then honest folk must do the same. Now that's simple enough."

"Yes."

"And what were you going to say?"

"I? Only nonsense."

"But all the same?"

"Oh nothing, only a trifle," said Natásha, smiling still more brightly. "I only wanted to tell you about Pétya: today nurse was coming to take him from me, and he laughed, shut his eyes, and clung to me. I'm sure he thought he was hiding. Awfully sweet! There, now he's crying. Well, good-by!" and she left the room.

Meanwhile downstairs in young Nicholas Bolkónski's bedroom a little lamp was burning as usual. (The boy was afraid of the dark and they could not cure him of it.) Dessalles slept propped up on four pillows and his Roman nose emitted sounds of rhythmic snoring. Little Nicholas, who had just waked up in a cold perspiration, sat up in bed and gazed before him with wide-open eyes. He had awaked from a terrible dream. He had dreamed that he and Uncle Pierre, wearing helmets such as were depicted in his Plutarch, were leading a huge army. The army was made up of white slanting lines that filled the air like the cobwebs that float about in autumn and which Dessalles called *les fils de la Vièrge*. In front was Glory, which was similar to those threads but rather thicker. He and Pierre were borne along lightly and joyously, nearer and nearer to their goal. Suddenly the threads that moved them began to slacken and become entangled and it grew difficult to move. And Uncle Nicholas stood before them in a stern and threatening attitude.

"Have you done this?" he said, pointing to some broken sealing wax and pens. "I loved you, but I have orders from Arakchéev and will kill the first of you who moves forward." Little Nicholas turned to look at Pierre but Pierre was no longer there. In his place was his father—Prince Andrew—and his father had neither shape nor form, but he existed, and when little Nicholas perceived him he grew faint with love: he felt himself powerless, limp, and formless. His father caressed and pitied him. But Uncle Nicholas came nearer and nearer to them. Terror seized young Nicholas and he awoke.

"My father!" he thought. (Though there were two good portraits of Prince Andrew in the house, Nicholas never imagined him in human form.) "My father has been with me and caressed me. He approved of me and of Uncle Pierre. Whatever he may tell me, I will do it. Mucius Scaevola burned his hand. Why should not the same sort of thing happen to me? I know they want me to learn. And I will learn. But someday I shall have finished learning, and then I will do something. I only pray God that something may happen to me such as happened to Plutarch's men, and I will act as they did. I will do better. Everyone shall know me, love me, and be delighted with me!" And suddenly his bosom heaved with sobs and he began to cry.

"Are you ill?" he heard Dessalles' voice asking.

"No," answered Nicholas, and lay back on his pillow.

"He is good and kind and I am fond of him!" he thought of Dessalles. "But Uncle Pierre! Oh, what a wonderful man he is! And my father? Oh, Father, Father! Yes, I will do something with which even *he* would be satisfied...."